How Love Grows

Triplets: Three Aren't One

Book Four

by

Dani Haviland

USA Today Bestselling Author

Copyright

Dedicated

This story is dedicated to families everywhere and of every type. Whether we were born into one, legally adopted, or claimed – forever may we remember and love one another!

Praise and Awards

"There wasn't a heartstring this one didn't pull at! And, no spoilers, but that's one of the nicest endings I could have imagined – all round, proving redemption's possible, some things will last forever, and …. Karma. This isn't just a story of Jose and Loren; it's so much more.   Amazon reader on *Too Fast for You* (http://bit.ly/2fast4YOU)

"From the picturesque descriptions of the Alaskan wilderness, to weaving a beautiful love story, the author's writing style is both serious and quirky. A perfect, relaxing read!"
    Amazon review of *One Arctic Summer* (http://bit.ly/2OneArcticSummer)

Chapter 1: Commitment

Mid-December 1991

"There you are, Dr. Buddy," the exuberant botanist declared, his hand outstretched in greeting. He looked around the desolate, snowy city park, making sure the two of them were alone. He continued, his voice now soft in case someone was eavesdropping. "Fifty-thousand dollars cash, just like you asked. I hope you don't mind that it's in an old valise. It's the only thing I had big enough to hold that much. Now, when are we going to get our baby?"

"Mr. Greene..." the obstetrician began, hoping his grimace of distaste at touching the cracked and sun-faded leather suitcase wasn't visible.

"Please, just call me Luther," the balding man said. "As in Luther Burbank."

"Ah, I see your parents had aspirations for you the moment you were born," the bootleg-baby doctor said, able to be more personable now that he felt the weight of the cash in his hand. "Your child is due in February but since it is one of a multiple-birth, I believe he or she will arrive early; say in a month or so. I have your contact information. I'll call as soon as the baby is ready to be picked up."

"So, you still don't know if we're getting a boy or girl?" Luther asked. "I thought you could detect the gender at five or six months gestation with ultrasounds."

"We can but since this is, shall we say, a private adoption, we prefer to remain out of and off the medical information system. We'd have to create a profile for the mother, record her personal information and more. We hold the privacy of our patients – both the unborn and the pregnant – in the highest regard."

"And the other baby is already spoken for by Gloria and Roger

1

Thornwhistle, correct?"

"Please, please, Mr. Greene," the doctor began, then noticing the distressed man's scowl, corrected himself. "Please, Luther, let's not use names. I'd prefer that you and the other adoptive parents never interacted. I'm not sure if these babies are identical, but if they are, there would be red flags raised about the adoption process."

"Huh?"

"If you were at a party with the other parents and you both had your children with you, don't you think there'd be questions about the relationship between the two youths if they were identical? Many of my clients prefer to claim the offspring as their biological children to avoid questions about how the adoption was transacted. I assure you, the mother has given her consent, but just in case she changes her mind later in life, don't you think she might want to see or reclaim her child, her children?"

"Oh, I never thought of that," Luther said, his face as pale as the leafless birch trees that surrounded them. "I guess it's time to move west."

"West, south, to Timbuktu, Africa – it really doesn't matter. I suggest you keep away from the northeastern portion of the United States, though. The other parents are prominent members of society. They'll certainly want their child to accompany them to many of the events they sponsor."

"Yeah," Luther said softly, still stunned at the idea of having to pull up roots. "My wife did say her old college roommate…" He took a deep breath to compose himself. "Her former sorority sister – who shall remain nameless – was quite active socially."

Dr. Buddy patted him on the shoulder, trying to calm the distressed man while keeping a tight banker's grip on the battered briefcase of cash. "Just make whatever arrangements you need to soon. You and your wife will be able to make a prosperous new start wherever you go, I'm sure." He lifted the money bag. "Who knows? Maybe you can find a way to make this grow on trees."

"Yeah, sure," Luther said glumly, then lifted his hands to blow warm air onto them. "Hey, I've taken enough of your time. I have to go. I forgot my gloves and don't want to get frostbitten."

Dr. Buddy patted his shoulder one more time before pulling his hand away. "You'll be getting a call from me in a month or two. Here's hoping for a safe delivery for mother and babies."

"Huh?"

"There's always a risk with childbirth," Dr. Buddy explained, biting back the smirk that was rising. "Whether the baby and mother survive or not, there are still costs involved. Didn't your wife tell you that this," he lifted the case of money, "is non-refundable?"

A chill ran up Luther's back. He tried to ignore the shiver of suspicion wrapped around his gut-clenching sense of evil foreboding, but the ominous pair of negative emotions were as palatable as his rising bile. "No, she didn't."

"I'm sure I mentioned it to the missus. I can't give out paper contracts for transactions of this personal nature, but I always make it a point to confirm my no refunds policy. If giving birth to a live baby was easy and one hundred percent assured, we wouldn't be meeting right now, would we?"

Jaws clenched to molar-grinding tightness so the rebuke he felt roiling didn't escape, Luther nodded that he had heard the doctor, then turned and walked away. Empty-handed and potentially empty-hearted in a month or two. How could the world be so full of promise one day, then teetering on the edge of disaster the next, knocked out of whack by greedy and manipulative monsters?

Yesterday, he had been burned and betrayed by his research partner. The unscrupulous over-educated monkey of a man rushed to D.C. as soon as they reran the test numbers, saying he was going out for lunch. He didn't waste even a moment to file for a patent. On the application, he claimed the innovative method and unique chemical elixir combination was the result of an epiphany and that he had performed the tests by himself and verified them with an independent lab. He left out that it was Luther's idea and they had done the experiments and research together over a course of months.

Now, the overgrown ape in a white jacket was sure to be the sole recipient of the millions of dollars the largest horticultural corporation in the western hemisphere had promised for the cloning technology.

As a result, he was one hundred percent clinically depressed. But, no matter how bummed he was, he had to roll out of bed and solve his monetary dilemma. A last-minute find of an adoptable infant had been brought to his wife's attention. Leanne's college roommate had called and said that for a *mere* $50,000, they could adopt a newborn from a woman who was clean, healthy, and never used drugs. She was only a few hours drive away. No dealing with airplanes, passports or government restrictions.

By the end of the afternoon, he'd pawned everything he could lay his hands on and cleaned out both their savings and retirement accounts. Yes, they were destitute. He'd even let go of his piano and first editions of Hemingway to get the cash to 'buy' the child that he'd been unable to create with his loving wife.

Now after meeting the doctor, he realized that this arrangement had all the markings of a scam. Whether the man was a licensed physician or not, he had the aura of a perpetually greedy devil, his eyes blazing with dollar lust.

All he had left in life were Leanne and hope. Hope that it wouldn't be the end of their love if the adoption fell through, too. He hadn't been able to give her the baby she'd wanted for twenty years. It didn't make a difference that she was the barren one, not him. Both of them had agreed to gamble on a backstreet adoption. They'd take the last of their money and cash in as much of their assets as was needed to start their family. Everything else was just stuff.

He ran his hand over the top of his bald head, wiping off the melted snow before he got back in the car. "I just hope my gut is wrong this time," he said, then put the key in the ignition. "Sometimes I hate it when I'm right."

4

"I know it's not much," Leanne said, bringing the platter out from the kitchen, "but I couldn't see spending all that money on a turkey when it's just the two of us. At least for a while. Just think... Any day now."

Luther watched his distracted wife set the dish too close to the edge of the plastic work table they'd been using to eat dinner on since they sold their oak drop-leaf table to invest in Dr. Buddy and the baby. "Watch what you're doing and stop gazing at the calendar," he said, pushing the plate closer to the center. "I promise, no matter how hard or long you stare at that numbered grid, it won't make time go faster. It's a constant."

"Hey, I have a degree, too," she snapped, then immediately became remorseful. "I'm sorry. I know I'm not pregnant, but sometimes I feel like I am. I mean, my moods are all over the place. The only thing worse is hearing myself apologize all the time because I've been bitching at you."

Luther picked up her hand and kissed it. "You may not be pregnant, dear wife, but you are expecting. Or as they say now, '*We* are expecting.'"

Leanne giggled at his grand gesture. "Yes, *we* are," she said. "Let me get the rest of the food. It may just be chicken, but it's a big one. I figure we should run out of meat about the same time that you're tired of chicken enchiladas or chicken soup."

"Or chicken salad or chicken and dumplings."

Leanne left the room and came back with a divided dish of mashed potatoes and peas and saw that Luther was now down in the dumps. He was mood-swinging again, too. She sat next to him, took his hand, and prayed. "Lord, I know you have great things planned for our new family. Thank You for helping us see that we don't need physical *stuff,* but only You and each other. Please guide us to where You want us. And thanks so much for our health and for keeping us together. Amen."

Luther squeezed her hand tight in response. "Thanks. I needed that. I sometimes lose focus. You're right, though. I'd give up every material object I own and the value of all my intellectual property to keep us together. I may not have a job, but I do have prospects. I was waiting to tell you until I had the final word on it, but I think I've lined up a position out west."

"West? How far?" Leanne said excitedly. "I'm ready to get away from all this ice and snow."

"How about Oregon?"

Her face fell. "Which part? I know it gets cold there, too."

"Willamette Valley – it's considered a Mediterranean climate. It's not much for winter chill but has long and dry summers. There are opportunities for growing dozens of different herbs, too. Lavender, mint, rosemary… Growing grapes would be fantastic but take a major financial investment. We'd have to work for someone else until we saved enough capital for our own venture."

"Our own vineyard…" Leanne mused. "A little bit of Italy on the west coast of America…"

"Or mint and lavender fields," Luther added. "The return on those would be sooner. We'll see. We may have to start in California. First things first: Christmas dinner!"

***

Ring! Ring!

"I got it! I got it!" Leanne shouted as she pushed the laundry basket out of her way.

Biting his lip, trying to keep the stomach-churning feeling of dread from turning into tears, Luther hugged the back of the door, staying partially hidden from his eager wife.

"Yes, this is she," she said, her face aglow. "Yes, I recognized your voice. Well, is it a boy or a girl? And when can we come to get her?"

The phone dropped from her hands and Luther rushed to catch her as her legs gave way. He verified she hadn't injured herself, then looked in her face, ready to ask what had happened. No words were needed, though. She couldn't have spoken even if he had asked. He picked up the phone as if it was radioactive, barely touching the hard plastic as he held it near his ear.

"Hello?" he asked. "Yes, this is Luther Greene. Oh, no; the mother, too? All three of them? There were four? Oh, three babies and the mother. Hey, thanks for calling, but I have to see to my wife. She's not doing too well right now. Bye."

"She's dead," Leanne babbled. "Dr. Buddy said our daughter was dead…"

"I know, I know, sweetheart. I talked to him, too." Luther sighed deeply, then decided to tell her his suspicions. "She might not be, though. I mean…"

Before he could finish the thought, Leanne had sprung back to life at the word *not*. "What do you mean?"

"I think Dr. Buddy's a con artist. I know he has a pregnant woman at his birthing center. He showed me a picture that he had snapped when she was sleeping. He even made sure the TV was on in the background so I could see the weather forecast on the news program. He wasn't lying about that. And she was huge! Yes, he probably wasn't lying about her having triplets, either. However, she didn't look sickly. He is a licensed obstetrician in New Hampshire – I verified that as soon as you told me Gloria was going to adopt a baby through a doctor's office. But when he took that money out of my hand last month… I swear, it was as if the devil's own was taking it. I guess I should have told you about my fears, but just in case it wasn't a scam, I decided to keep it to myself."

"So, what do we do?" Leanne asked, focused on picking up the laundry she had knocked over, concentrating on something she was in control of.

"Call Gloria and see if she got the same call," he said. "Do you want to or do you want me to?"

"I got this," she said, setting down the basket. "I may not have my baby, but I do have hope."

Leanne dialed her friend's number, then hung up and retried. "It's busy. Maybe she's talking to that bastard, Buddy."

Luther chuckled, glad that rage had overtaken her grief. If it had to be one of the two strong emotions, he'd take the rage. Nothing was sadder than a wife who couldn't get up off the couch because of depression.

"There she is!" she finally said, then closed her eyes to concentrate on the call that was going through. "Hi, Gloria? Yes, did you get a call… No, wait! Don't fret or fall apart or whatever you want to call it. At least, not yet. Luther seems to think that Dr. Buddy is scamming us. Yes, there's a good chance the babies are fine. Shoot! I don't know. Maybe he has a dozen people he's promising those babies to. Yes, I know. I saw the same pictures. Don't you think that he could just as well have shown them to twelve people as two? Okay. Well, right now, I'm going to pray and I suggest you do, too. Don't you have a friend who's a private detective or something? Okay, so he does it as a hobby. Maybe this guy Silas can help us out. Yes, keep in touch. Those first words literally knocked me off my feet, but Luther caught me. I'm sure we'll get our babies eventually. Okay. I love you, too."

"Well?" Luther asked.

"You make phone calls if you need to, I'm going to find every candle in this house, then get down on my hands and knees and pray for a miracle."

"Frankly, dear, I don't care which one of us gets an answer first as long as it's that we have a daughter, waiting for Mama and Papa to come to get her."

"Amen to that!"

***

"Gloria, this is Chuck. Hey, I have great news. I just helped deliver three small but beautiful and healthy baby girls. I know we should wait a few hours, but I thought you might want to come and get yours early. What? No, she didn't die. No! Nobody died. All three babies are fine and so is the mother. Who told you that? Oh, he's in so much trouble already and why I wanted you to come early, but this is worthy of an expedited ticket to hell. No, do not call him back and give him a piece of your mind or contact him about anything else ever again. He's about an hour away from getting busted for white slavery, kidnapping, racketeering, and probably a whole bucketload of other charges. You have to get here fast, though. Remember that gas station mini-market where you dropped me off last month after our shopping trip at the mall? Right, that's it. Get there, stat. Do not stop for anything other than to call the other parents. I don't have your friend's number but if Buddy told you the girls died, I'm pretty sure he told that to everyone else he'd contracted with for delivery of a newborn. I don't know what to say to them because I don't know who they are. I do know you, though. Hey, I gotta go. Oh, and the password is Woodstock. I'll be driving my new old white work van. *Ciao*!"

Gloria set the phone down, tears streaming from her eyes.

"Are you all right?" Roger asked, holding her tight. "Don't worry, I know it deep down in my bones that we'll get a child one of these days. Hopefully soon, but I know…"

Holding her hand up to ask him to stop his babbling, Gloria nodded. "Hold that thought." She picked up the phone again and dialed Leanne.

"Hey, sweetheart. It's me, Gloria. Yes, I got the same phone call from Dr. Buddy, but don't you believe a word he said! You and Luther put on a coat and drive to that little gas station convenience store at Hemingway and Sherlock. Our daughters will be there! Yes, they're alive! Now get going! We don't want to be late!"

"Wha… What's that all about?"

"Roger, grab your keys and I'll explain on the way." Gloria looked around the huge foyer with a renewed vision. Yes, it was a grand mansion by anyone's standards, but in a few minutes, it would be their daughter's home.

"Leanne!" Gloria squealed as she ran into her friend's open arms. "Dr. Buddy lied to us. They're all fine. Nobody died and we still get the babies. Are you ready for this?"

"I've been ready for this since I was three and playing with rag dolls," Leanne said with a feigned frown. She shrugged her shoulders in excitement and started hopping up and down, her joy uncontainable.

Luther moved around the ladies and shook Roger's hand. "Can you believe this?"

"Not yet," Roger answered, his tone reserved. He shook his head, trying to remain the calm and sensible person of the group. Suddenly his smile popped free, his anticipation overriding doubt. "Oh, I am so ready!" he said with unrestrained excitement.

A silver vehicle pulled up to the fuel island on the opposite side of the station from them and all heads turned.

"Is that them?" Gloria asked, clinging to her husband's arm as she stood on tiptoes, trying for a better look.

Roger gave her hand a comforting pat, then moved away from the group so he could see who it was. "I don't know. Did he tell you what he'd be driving?"

"Oh, yeah. He said he'd be driving a white van," Gloria said. "Remember the password, 'Woodstock.'"

"Sounds like my kind of guy," Luther remarked. He hugged his wife around the shoulders. "Remember when we were there?"

"How could I forget," Leanne said, then giggled. "Over twenty years ago, and now our baby is finally here. That's a long gestation!"

"There's Chuck!" Gloria exclaimed, hopping up and down with joy, her hands tucked under her chin at seeing his familiar face behind the steering wheel.

"Settle down," Roger said. "You don't want to bring attention to us."

"Two middle-aged couples, snuggled up against the wind,

looking like vultures ready to pounce… I'd say we were already suspicious," Luther said.

The driver of the van looked beyond the gas pumps and saw the two couples standing by the stack of bundled firewood, their smiles of anticipation marking them as the new parents. Chuck rolled past them and came to a stop at the side of the mini-store, out of sight of anything but owls searching for dinner. "Tranquility base: Stork One and Stork Two have landed," he said to his new companion, then opened the door and got out.

"Hey, there," the perky young doctor said as he approached the huddled foursome. "Anyone for a game of golf? Know a good course around here?"

"How about Woodstock?" Gloria said, then ran up to Chuck and gave him a big hug. "Are they inside? Are they okay? I thought I was going to have a total meltdown when Dr. Buddy called and said that Grace had died and they couldn't get the babies out in time. That they had all passed."

Chuck's eyes widened. "Grace was alive when I left." He opened the side door, exposing his new traveling nursemaid and the gym bag full of babies.

"I'm still alive," Grace Two said indignantly, then groaned softly as she realized it was a misunderstanding about the shared name. "I think you'd better call me Nanny." She looked at the eager parents crowded around the open door, the women squeezed in front of their husbands to keep away from the chill. "Why don't you ladies come inside?"

Gloria led the way. "Which one is ours?" she asked once inside, peering into the unzipped bag.

"It's up to you two who gets Aqua and who gets Pinkie," Chuck said, watching the allocation of babies from the front seat. "The yellow-wrapped sweetheart is mine."

"Oh, my God!" Leanne exclaimed. "They *are* identical! I can't believe it. How will we know whose is whose?"

Little Pinkie opened her eyes, started to squall, then caught sight of Gloria and smiled. "I don't care if she's the biggest or not; this one's mine."

"Then that must mean she's ours. Oh, I can't believe it. I swear I feel a tingling in my breasts. I'm as barren as a moon rock, but I swear she's kicked in a bucket load of estrogen." Leanne looked at the dark-haired young woman who'd been taking care of the babies. "Can I take her home now?"

"That's the plan. Oh, and don't even try to get in touch with Dr. Buddy. Either of you. If they didn't catch him, they will. You're lucky Chuck and I got in the middle of this or you wouldn't be celebrating motherhood tonight."

"Thank you, Nanny?" Gloria said, unsure of her name. "Chuck has my number. If you two run into any trouble or need a few bucks, just give me a call." She unzipped her jacket and put the swaddled baby inside. "Come on Vickie. You're coming home."

Leanne copied Gloria's tactic of kangaroo-pouch carrying the baby in the coat. "And you, too, Tori Lynn. Daddy's waiting outside."

Leanne stepped out of the van, then suddenly yipped. "She latched on! Oh, my Lord! I'm going to see if Luther can set me up with some of those plant estrogens. I may be able to nurse my baby still! Sing hallelujah!"

Chapter 2: New Beginnings

January 3, 1992

The young mother, now devoid of the babies she'd carried for eight months, was distraught at her loss. She'd made a decision, though, and for eight long months had believed it was right. Her best friend in the world had tried the whole time she'd known she was pregnant to talk her into keeping her babies, knowing that between him and their extended family, they could keep her evil mother out of the babies' lives, but she wouldn't believe him.

Now it was too late. The babies were dead and it was all her fault. If she'd chosen a traditional hospital, they might have detected the problem sooner and been able to take the babies in time. They'd all be alive. Even if she had signed away her parental rights and couldn't get them back, they'd be living – loving and being loved by parents somewhere.

What was it that Dr. Buddy said was the problem? Grace shook her head, all her memories a jumble of random words and technical mumbo jumbo, twisted and skewed by the residual sedatives still in her system. His explanation still didn't make sense. Would it ever?

Chuck? Where had he been during these last hours? She blinked back her tears of loss. She had sent him away, using harsh words she could never take back. The man had stood by her for months. Pretended to be her lover if needed, given up his family and his medical career to protect her away from her vile and vindictive mother. And she'd returned his caring with curses and scorn. What kind of scum was she to treat a generous and caring man like that?

Grace's shoulder twinged in discomfort. The subconscious pain always came when she thought of her. What kind of mother would shoot her own daughter? It couldn't even be considered a crime of passion since she had done it in cold blood. Thank God her reflexes were quick and she ducked in time to save herself from death at the close-range firing. Still, she'd need to watch out for the woman's

13

sudden reappearance.

"Gracie, do you want something to eat or drink?" Dusty asked.

But I'm safe now. Dusty's back in my life. Mother wasn't able to scare him away.

"Something to drink," Grace said. "Maybe water?"

"Get her some chocolate milk and pick up a gallon of water, too. She needs some calories and we all could use the water," Papa Doc said.

And I have Papa Doc, Daddy, and Silas, too. Between those four men who love me so much, maybe I'll be safe...

Grace snuggled into her father's jacket, inhaling his familiar scent. *How could I ever believe he wouldn't protect me. I've been such a fool.*

A gush of cold air came into the cab of the truck. She looked up. They were at a gas station and Dusty had his hands full. When had that happened? Time was skewed – as shattered and scattered as a thousand-piece jigsaw puzzle thrown across a rock garden.

"Here you go, Mr. Stillwater."

She looked up to the voice. Dusty was handing a jug of drinking water and a carton of chocolate milk to her father. *Yes, Dusty still wanted her. Did he know what she'd done? What she'd been through? About the other man she'd been with? If he didn't know and found out, would it change his mind?*

Her father speaking to Dusty brought her back to reality. "Seeing as you've been through so much hell and still seem pretty set on marrying my daughter, you can go ahead and call me Dad or Hal, whichever feels more comfortable."

Beep! Beep!

Confused and afraid that she might be hallucinating, Grace sat up and looked for the source of the roadrunner's chirp.

"What was that?" Dusty asked, looking around.

"My cell phone," Papa Doc said. "I got what they call a personalized alert tone for my incoming texts." He took the phone out of his shirt pocket, tapped a few buttons, and then put it back. He looked at Hal and grimaced. "Someone just checking to make sure all went well on our end," and nodded at Grace.

"It's going to take time for all of us to heal," she heard her father say. "Some losses take longer to get over. Let's hope you haven't lost Chuck because of all of this."

Chuck! Where is he? Did she send him away forever? What had she said?

"Only for a little time," Papa Doc said. "My son has a nurturing soul and is a gentleman. I think he's just stepping back so Dusty can help her heal."

"What do you mean?" Hal asked.

Daddy sounds confused. He's not the only one!

"Chuck didn't know Dusty was coming with us or that we even found him. That was last minute, remember?"

Does Chuck even know Dusty by sight? No, they've never met; although I did mention him a few million times in the last eight months.

"Yeah, I wouldn't know your son if I sat on him," Dusty said. "Hey, does anyone want some chocolate?"

Grace tried to quiet her persistent doubts and focused on the sounds of her men bantering back and forth, their voices rising and lowering with their emotions and concerns. She hadn't heard her father and two surrogate uncles in a month and didn't realize until now how much she had missed them.

And Dusty. He was here now, safe from her mother's false accusations.

She looked out the window. The world was getting better, itty bit by itty bit. The man she had gone through hell for was here. Would Dusty accept her as she was? The way he had held her – and sobbed uncontrollably with joy – when he rescued her after she had been abandoned by Nurse Ellen, she knew he'd do anything for her. He seemed to be sharing her feeling of loss for the babies, too. All her men could mourn with her. And they would heal together, too.

Everyone is here but Chuck. Where is he? She closed her eyes tight and tried to find a thread of recent memory, struggling to recall the last words he had said to her. There it was. An echo of his voice. He was leaving her, he said – leaving so she wouldn't associate him with her loss.

Which would have been worse, the loss of the babies to adoption or death? Definitely death. With adoption, they would still have been happy little people with families who cared for and cherished them. Now with death, they were just little corpses. Was it her fault they had died? Did she do something wrong?

Grace looked at Dusty, blinking back the tears that had returned. A familiar movement out of the corner of her eye caught her attention. She leaned over him to watch the man coming out of the convenience store. "Who's that?" she asked, pointing out the window.

Dusty recognized him as the man he had swapped jugs of water with earlier. "Just some guy from the store. He got coffee and water, too. Why? Do you know him?"

She sighed then leaned back into his arm. "I thought I did…"

He's alive and moving on with his life. I should, too.

"Grace, I know it's not exactly romantic – my timing and all," Dusty said.

She turned to him, warmed by his presence. She felt a smile rise, the first one in ages.

"But I want to make a new life with you as my wife," he said and put his arm around her to snuggle her close. "I have a lot going on now. I have my own business and everything. I still want to marry you and always will. We can start again with a family as soon as you say the word. I kinda know what went on with the other guy, and it doesn't matter to me. I mean, I know you have been hurt in about a million different ways, but I want to help you heal. Would you let me? I mean, I'll do it however you want, but I'd rather do it as your husband than as your best friend."

16

Grace leaned into him further and inhaled his unique scent of boy and man. She felt his nearness light up her face. She looked up. "Yeah, I think I'd like you better as a husband. Let me get healed up, and then let's get married. But if you don't mind, I'd still like to live with Papa Doc and Silas for a while. And hang out with my dad, too."

"And me?"

"Duh! You'd be living with us, too. One great big dysfunctional family."

***

"Leanne, are you sure you want to try this tea? I mean, it won't hurt you but it might make you a bit moody." Luther lifted the teapot with his concoction of fenugreek, fennel, and half a dozen other herbs. "And it might taste nasty, too, but should help amplify your body's own trace amounts of oxytocin and help with milk production."

"I'll try anything, even though I think I could probably do it with only the stimulation of her suckling or whatever those fancy words are for making milk." Leanne poured out a cup of the pale brew and guzzled it down. "Do I taste ginger in that?"

"Just a few slivers in the whole pot. I didn't think it would hurt, plus if the other herbs upset your tummy, it would help."

Luther looked into the dresser drawer he had lined with towels and scarves and saw that his little five-pound blessing was awake and squirming. "Ready to try again?"

Leanne sat down in the rocker – one of the few pieces of furniture they hadn't sold – and bared a breast. "Yes, I am. She's tiny and doesn't need much to start. I'm glad I read up on how much babies need to eat. We may not have formula, but Lord willing, we'll be successful right out of the chute and never have to buy any."

"And Mama-made will be easier when we're on the road," Luther added.

Leanne winced at the sudden contact. "Man, she can suck!" she whispered emphatically, keeping her volume down so she didn't startle the blonde baby.

"Our little Tori Lynn Greene," Luther said, tears coming to his eyes. "I've never seen anything so beautiful as my wife nursing our child."

Sniff. Sniff. "Now you got me going, too," Leanne said, then paused. "Oh, my God! That's what they're talking about! I swear, my milk just let down. Whoosh! The sensation is indescribable but real. Oh, we are so doing this, little one." She looked up at her husband and added. "Papa."

"I used to think I wanted to be called Dad or Daddy, but when you say it, Papa sounds so right. Yup, Papa it is."

***

Two months later

"Are you sure it isn't too early in the year to be heading west?" Leanne asked for the third time since breakfast.

Rather than answer, Luther looked her way and scowled.

"I'm sorry. I know it's the right choice. I'm just scared to death of snowstorms and flat tires and…"

"Leanne, where's your faith? We've seen so many miracles in our lives, overcome so many obstacles, and you still doubt?"

"I know, I know," she said, then looked down at the map again. "Are you sure you want to go all the way to California? Wouldn't Texas be closer?"

"Maybe, but there are more diverse horticultural opportunities available in California. Besides, I hear they're thinking of making marijuana legal there soon. I'd love to get in on the ground floor of that industry."

"That'll happen when pigs fly," Leanne said. "And no, don't even think of doing any underground or black market growing or selling or…"

Luther put his hand on his wife's arm. "I'd never do anything illegal or risky. I got out of growing that when I married you. What makes you think I'd risk arrest or imprisonment with you two depending on me?"

Leanne put her hand on top of his. "I never thought you would. It's just you have such a gift of making plants thrive. Not many men can just look at a plant and see what it needs. I'm sure we'll find the right employer for you once we get to California. If you can do that for annuals, I'm sure you can do it for grapes and other perennials, too."

"And if I don't care for all the rules and restrictions they have in the Golden State, we can always venture north a bit. Lots of green in Oregon!"

"A lavender farm. Now that sounds interesting…" Leanne mused, sniffing the hand lotion on the back of her hand. "A cottage industry of creating handmade soaps and lotions…"

"Sounds like a lot of work," Luther said. "Let me try to use more brains and less brawn to make a living. I'm not getting any younger. Let's save your passion for sweet-smelling botanicals to crafting, not selling retail or wholesale."

"At least until Tori's older and doesn't take so much of my time." She noticed Luther's look of confusion. "Not that I'm complaining. I've had twenty years to cook, craft, and sew. I'll be back to doing more of those in a flash, wondering what I should do with so much time on my hands."

"Yup, these are the good old days," Luther said. "Enjoy them."

***

April 1994

"That's it – we're moving!" Luther announced as he walked in the front door of the ramshackle converted chicken coop he and his family had lived in for two years.

"How soon?" Leanne asked, looking around to see how much trouble it would be to pack up. When she realized there was nothing she cared about other than her family and a plastic tote of their 'treasures,' she smiled broadly and added, "Do we want to go tonight or wait until morning?"

"I do love you so, wife," he said and held her close. He looked around the room as she had with the same 'what do I need to pack' attitude and wondered why he had waited for two years to see if life growing mint as a sharecropper would ever get better.

"I'm sorry I kept us here so long," he said. "I really did think that everything would turn around. If only I hadn't been robbed of my patents…"

"The toilets of the world are overflowing with the crap that 'if only,' regrets, and looking back are made of. Knock it off. Face forward!"

"Crap! Face Forward!" two-year-old Tori said, looking up from her favorite toy: an interactive four-sided rotating plastic cube.

"Sometimes I wish she hadn't started talking," Luther said.

Leanne chuckled. "Yup, she's a genius at picking out the key points in a conversation, that's for sure."

"She has all she needs for toys with that thing," Luther said, bending down to play with her. He picked up the cube and looked at the mirror side. "Where's Tori?"

"Babies!" she said, grabbing for it, bouncing in place with glee.

"Do you think she remembers that she had two sisters?" Luther asked, trying not to frown.

Leanne stared at her child, visualizing two babies who looked just like her sitting next to her. She blinked and the image was gone. "I don't know. Maybe I'll ask her when she's old enough to understand. I know that every once in awhile, I see all three."

"No, don't ask her. It will only complicate her life. Let's keep everything simple. How about you make some sandwiches and we take off tonight? We can sleep in the back of the station wagon."

"Blankets, bologna, our box, and our baby. Yup, moving day is simple. Are you going to leave a note or call?"

"Call who? No one's checked on us in six months. Nah, we don't owe anyone and I'm not going to harvest anything, so there's no income lost or due. Let's head south. Even if I have to take a job as an itinerant fruit picker, we'll be fine. We may have to live on nectarines and strawberries for a while, but we'll be fine, I know it."

"I know it, too."

"Strawberries!" Tori said.

***

January 3, 1997

"She's five years old today," Leanne said. "So big compared to when she was born…"

"And old enough for public school next year," Luther said. "They probably would have made an exemption for her and let her enroll early because she could read already."

"I know, but I'm not ready for her to leave me. I mean, if I thought they could teach her something I couldn't, I'd let her go."

"No, you wouldn't," Luther said, one eyebrow raised.

Leanne looked up and saw the gesture that meant 'I won't let you win this one, no matter how much you want to argue. Go ahead and give up now because you know I'm right.'

"What can they teach her that I can't?" she asked, unwilling to admit defeat without at least a discussion on the subject.

"School will teach her how to get along with others, how to interact and carry on a conversation with someone her age who isn't imaginary. Good grief; how to play team sports, turn somersaults and cartwheels…"

"You're probably right," Leanne agreed, frowning in defeat.

"Don't be sad, Mama," Tori said. She walked over and stood next to her mother's chair. She put her arm around her mother's neck and snuggled her close. "You're doing a great job teaching me. Knowing how to turn somersaults and cartwheels won't help me develop a more efficient energy source or create a cleaner environment."

"Good Lord, Tori!" Luther exclaimed. "What have you been reading?"

Tori picked up the latest scientific trade magazine her mother had brought home from the recycling center. It was a year old but new to her. "This."

21

He rolled his eyes and shook his head in amazement.

"Okay, I see what you mean. School doesn't start for a few days, though," Leanne said.

"Winter break ended today. Tori, do you want to go to school with other kids? They might be a bit boring at first, but I'm sure you'll find things to do with them that your mother and I can't."

"Like turn somersaults and cartwheels?" she asked.

"Among other things. Going to school will be a brand new universe for you to explore, interacting with people who have different perspectives and interests in life..."

Tori set her hand on her father's and, paraphrasing Renée Zellweger's classic line, said, "You had me at brand new."

***

The next day was brisk, even for a California winter day. "Ready for school?" Luther asked.

"Her or me?" replied Leanne.

"Both. Either."

"She's fine. I'm a mess," Leanne said. She ran the brush through her hair one more time, noting that it was now more salt than pepper. "Do you think I should color it?"

"Absolutely not," Luther replied, then kissed the top of her head. "I love your silver highlights. Mark my words; platinum locks will be the new golden tresses in a few years. I don't want you changing your looks for anyone, even you. You're perfect. You're the best you that can possibly be."

Leanne giggled, remembering the night before. They were in their fifties but were as frisky and passionately in love as they had been in their twenties.

"Is this what kids wear to school?" Tori asked, walking into their room.

Luther swallowed the laugh, but Leanne couldn't help herself and chuckled at the comical combination of styles. "No, honey. I don't think they wear jeans and a tutu at the same time."

"Why not? It's almost freezing today. You make me wear pants when it's cold," she said, rubbing her hand down the side of her denims, "but it's also my first day of school and I want to look pretty." She spun around and showed off the handmade skirt of pink nylon net.

"Yes, dear," Leanne explained as gently as she could. "But wearing a fairy princess dress might be a little too much. Let's just stay with blue jeans and a flannel shirt."

"Fine! But don't blame me if they can't tell if I'm a boy or a girl."

"What?" Leanne and Luther asked at the same time.

"Because my hair is short," Tori said, her head hung down in shame.

"Oh, sweetheart," Luther said, holding her close. "You're beautiful whether your hair is long or short. I thought you liked it short so it didn't tangle."

Tori's glower would have been comical if she hadn't been so distraught.

"How about I put a ribbon in it?" Leanne asked. "Boys never wear those."

Nodding as she thought about it, Tori said with a sincerity beyond her tender years, "Let's make it a pink ribbon, just to be sure."

"Pink it is."

***

Luther and Leanne drove up to the front of the elementary school, chilly from both anticipation and the cold north wind. "This is such a big step in our little girl's life."

"Our life, too," Luther added. "Next thing you know, we'll be helping her pick out a wedding dress."

Unbidden tears suddenly burst forth from Leanne, but she caught them with a hankie. "Danged allergies," she said as she wiped them away.

"It's the wrong time of year for hay fever," Tori said. "And it's okay to cry. Don't fear the unknown: embrace it!" she added, sniffing back her own tears of apprehension.

"Oh, my!" Leanne said. She looked at Luther. "What have we done?"

Luther had been thinking the same thing. Their daughter's philosophy on life was at least ten years beyond that of others her age. Is this why nature didn't give older people children? Did they teach them too much too soon?

"Sweetheart," Luther said, holding Tori by her shoulders, looking deep into her eyes. "These other children might not have had parents who shared as much with them as we do with you. Try to use smaller words."

"You mean monosyllabic not a lesser-sized font, right?" she asked, ending her question with a wink.

"Just give them a chance, and whatever you do, don't try to make someone feel dumb. That's cruel and we're not mean people."

"Yeah, mean people suck. Can we go in now? People are staring at us."

Luther and Leanne looked up and saw little faces peering out the window, two adult women behind them, watching the pensive family having their last chit chat before coming in. "The start of a new year and a new phase in your life."

"Our lives," Leanne whispered. "My days are going to be so empty."

Chapter 3: Adjustment Period

"Mr. and Mrs. Greene and Tori Lynn," the school secretary read, looking over the application. "So, you adopted her or are you her guardians?"

"Excuse me?" Leanne asked indignantly, not even trying to hide her anger.

"Oh, I'm sorry. I thought you had legal custody of her in some way." She looked up at Leanne's gray hair, then ran her fingers through her own silvery locks. "We're a little old to be biological parents of kindergartners."

"Speak for yourself," Leanne hissed, her eyes narrowed and fists clenched at her side.

"What my wife is saying is what difference does it make to you or the school or anyone else? If there's a medical emergency and she needs a blood transfusion or a kidney, we'll let the medical professionals take care of that. My concern is that *my* daughter won't languish in the classrooms; that the teachers will be able to offer her intellectual stimulation and challenges."

"Oh, don't worry about that, Mr. Greene. Some of our kinder-kids can already read."

"That's *Dr.* Greene," Luther said. "I'm a botanist. And Tori can already read and perform basic math computations."

Leanne cleared her throat and nudged Luther. He clarified his remark. "Tori can read way beyond the first-grade level and perform advanced mathematical computations."

"You know, it's not always good to teach a child beyond her age," the secretary admonished, making sure she kept her eyes focused on her paperwork, not engaged with the elderly couple who were so proud of their prodigy.

Luther grabbed Leanne's clenched fist. "At least one day," he whispered. "Let's give it at least one day…"

Her hand relaxed into his. "Okay."

"Now, if Tori is ready," the secretary said, standing up and facing the trio, "let's go introduce all of you to her teacher and the aide."

"Excuse me," Tori said. She pointed to the woman's enamel lapel pin. "Are you from Latvia?"

"What? Why yes! How'd you know?" She looked down at the colorful pin with a single rhinestone and verified what she already knew: the country name wasn't on it. "Do you know what this little jewel signifies?"

"First, I knew because the shape of the pin looks like Latvia. Second, I'm not sure, but that jewel looks like it's where Riga would be. It might be a suburb, though. I don't know the names of all the cities."

Leanne beamed with parental pride. There was no reason to tell the self-righteous secretary that Latvia was her native country nor that they had a stylized map of it in their living room.

The group entered the small and tidy classroom, the walls lined with plastic and wicker baskets filled with assorted toys and shelves of colorful picture books. The floors were covered with patchwork mats and rugs decorated with pictures of farms and roads. The whole area gave off a warm, homey vibe, assuring the hesitant parents that they had made the right decision. There was so much to offer their daughter in this room. Outdoor activities, crafts, and the library would certainly enhance Tori's life experience way beyond what the two of them and their limited resources could offer.

The introductions to the teacher, aide, and the class as a whole went well, so Luther and Leanne bade Tori farewell, comfortable that no harm would come to their little girl.

"Do you think they'll let us come back and have lunch with her?" Leanne asked Luther on the way back to the car.

"You're going to have to cut the cord sometime, dear. Let her try this out her own way. She'll never be able to stand on her own two feet if you keep clutching her so close to you."

She looked at her watch. "All right. But I want to get here fifteen

26

minutes before school's out to pick her up just in case there's a crowd."

"Come on, wife," Luther said, his arm around her shoulder. "I think I have something that will take your mind off of her. It's been a while since we had alone time in the middle of the day. I took the whole day off work, so the next five hours are just for you and me."

"Well, maybe you will and maybe you won't distract me, but it will be fun trying!"

***

"You can hang your backpack on the hook at the number fifteen," Mrs. Johnson said. "That's one and five. Do you know your numbers?"

Tori grinned, remembering that she wasn't supposed to make anyone feel dumb. Papa had said the kids, but he probably meant the teacher, too. "Yes, ma'am."

And then she couldn't help herself. "It's the digit one and the digit five – both prime numbers – not the sum of one and five which would be six, which is not a prime number. And neither is fifteen. A prime number, that is. It is the product of two primes, though: three and five."

The teacher looked around the room to see if the other students were paying attention to their conversation. They weren't. They were gathered around the terrarium, intent on watching the tarantula consume its meal of young crickets. "I like numbers, too," she said. "They're kind of like a foreign language to most five-year-old students, though. Maybe you'd better only chat about prime numbers with me."

Tori nodded, glad that she had already made a friend. Maybe Mrs. Johnson could teach her how to turn somersaults. Nah. She was as old as Mama. She'd probably have to learn that from another kid.

"What are they doing?" she asked before hanging up her backpack.

"We have a classroom pet. It's a big hairy spider. It's lunchtime for Mr. Tarantula. Do you want to watch him eat?"

"Spiders don't have hair, they have setae which look like hair but aren't made of protein," Tori said, then noticed the wide-eyed stare that always meant she'd shared too much. "But they sure look like hairs, huh?"

"Yes, they do. Why don't you use your first day here just to observe? Just like if you were researching in the field, you'd want to watch your subjects in their natural habitat before coming to any conclusions about what they're doing or why." Mrs. Johnson lifted up the backpack to put it on the hook. "This is terribly heavy. Is there something breakable in here?"

"Only if you drop it," Tori said, then took the bag and finished setting it on the hook carefully.

The rest of the morning went smoothly, Tori watching her peers as they stacked blocks, strung colored beads, and cut out paper circles. Rather than create her own intricate patterns and designs, she intentionally scaled back her talents, mimicking the others so she didn't stand out. *Now I know how Jane Goodall felt when she interacted with gorillas! You don't have to be smarter or stronger or prove anything! This is fun.*

Finally, it was lunchtime. She took out her colorful cloth lunch bag and the wax-paper wrapped sandwich and apple and sat down at a table by herself, waiting to see if someone would join her. A minute later, the freckle-faced red-haired boy who had been staring at her all morning sat down beside her. He set his action hero lunch box down and opened it up, displaying his plastic packets of sugary snacks and a juice box.

"What do you have for lunch? If it's good, we can trade," he said, peering past her boring homemade-bread sandwich see what was in her cloth bag.

"Oh, that's not to eat," she said. She stood up so she could use both hands and lifted out the canning jar filled with water and a goldfish.

"Ew! Is that what you're eating for lunch?" he asked.

"Ew!" echoed the other kids at the adjoining table.

"Sushi!" someone said and laughed.

"No, her name is Suzy, not Sushi," Tori said. "She's my pet, not my lunch." She looked at the plastic-wrapped processed food the redhead had wanted to swap and shook her head. "And thanks but no thanks. I don't eat that kind of junk. Do you know how long it takes for that plastic to decompose in the landfill?"

"Huh?" he asked.

"Never mind. Let's just eat our own food." Tori leaned close to the jar and looked at the fish. "I think you'd better stay home tomorrow, Suzy. This isn't as much fun as I thought it'd be."

After they finished lunch, the other students started disappearing. Tori put her fish back in the bag and went to Mrs. Johnson. "Where did they go?"

"Oh, I'm sorry, Tori. I forgot to tell you. After lunch, you're free to go outside and play on the playground until twelve-fifteen. There's the clock. I'll bet you already know how to tell time, don't you?"

"Yes, ma'am. But would you watch Suzy for me? I'm afraid she might get kicked over if I take her outside."

"Sure thing, sweetheart." She took the quart jar and verified there were air holes in the top. Of course, there were. She held it close, protecting the little girl's treasured pet. She'd have to talk to her parents. Tori was a precious jewel. If she hung out with traditional kids full time, though, she'd lose her shine. One day a week would probably be enough to keep up with her social skills. Any more than that and she'd become dull and common or pick up bad habits. She definitely wanted to keep up with this little one.

After recess, Mrs. Johnson gave the drill as the children began to come in from outside. "Okay, line up. If you have to use the bathroom, do it now. If you don't, still go in and wash your hands," she said.

"It's this way," a little dark-haired girl said, taking Tori by the elbow.

29

Tori walked into the restroom and was stunned. So many mirrors! Bypassing the toilets and sinks, she went into the corner where two mirrors intersected, providing an infinity perspective. "Wow!"

"Pretty awesome, huh?" Melinda said. "It's like there's a whole bunch of you."

Tori reached out with both hands and touched each mirror, her eyes staring as if in a trance.

"Are you going to be okay?" Melinda asked. "You look kind of spooky."

"It's like there's more than three of me. It's like there are hundreds and hundreds…"

"Come on," Melinda said, "they're not going anywhere. You can go potty first and I'll wait for you. We don't want to be late for storytime."

"Bye, bye," Tori said softly to the images. "Nice seeing you again."

***

"There she is," Leanne said, pointing her out at the end of the line of youngsters.

"Our little girl looks so grown up with her backpack…and is she frowning?" Luther asked.

"If you can't tell, then you need glasses, Papa. Don't say anything. Let her talk to us first."

"Be careful," Tori said, handing her mother the pack. "I brought Suzy to school today, so don't spill her."

"You brought your goldfish to school?" Luther asked. "I'm sorry. That's what you just said, isn't it?"

"I thought she'd like it, but she didn't. Can she stay home with you tomorrow?"

"Yes, dear. We'll take good care of her," Leanne said.

"And can I stay home with her?"

"What? Don't you like school?" Luther asked. He felt his wife's glare of disapproval but ignored it. "You know, sometimes first

30

impressions aren't right. I figured it would take you up to a week to like school."

"Oh, I like the school and the teacher and some of the kids, but they called me crazy. I'm not crazy, though. I saw my sisters today, and maybe I shouldn't have told Melinda, but I thought she could keep a secret."

Luther slammed on the brakes at the revelation, thrusting all of them forward. "Sorry. My foot slipped," he said, then quickly glanced at Leanne to see her reaction.

Yes, she was just as stunned. They both looked at Tori, waiting for her to elaborate.

"They were both there, wearing the same hair ribbon and everything. Both of them!" she said, not even trying to contain her elation.

"Whoa, wait!" Luther said. "You said you have two sisters and you saw them today? Where?"

"See, you didn't say I didn't have two sisters. You asked where."

"Tori Lynn…" Leanne said, her voice low with her no-nonsense intonation.

"They were in the back of the mirror. Both of them!"

Luther and Leanne both exhaled in relief at the same time. "You were looking at your own reflection, sweetheart. You don't have a sister hiding in the back of a mirror."

"Sisters," she said in an authoritative voice. "There were two of them and they looked just like me. I promise."

"And I promise to teach you about mirrors and the principle of light refraction and reflection this afternoon as soon as we get home."

"Mama can come into the girls' bathroom with me tomorrow and see. I'll prove it."

"Or we can use a hand mirror in our bathroom mirror and show you the same thing at home. Just because you see more than one image doesn't mean there is more than one person. Can you imagine if there was a flesh and blood person behind every reflective image?

31

There wouldn't be enough food in the world to feed everyone."

"Okay, I'll let you show me your side of the story, but I know I have two sisters."

Tori watched as her parents shared a guilty look then turned back to watching the road in silence. Maybe they were right about reflective surfaces and images and the world getting too crowded if there were real people on the other side, but she knew as sure as she was breathing air and not water that she had sisters.

But she also knew she'd never mention it again. She didn't like her parents pretending they didn't know. Or being called crazy.

Chapter 4: The Compassionate Use Act

July 3, 1997

"Happy birthday, sweetheart!" Luther and Leanne sang out.

Tori rubbed the sleep out of her eyes, then did a double-take at the colorful bicycle sitting in the middle of the living room. "It's not my birthday."

"Well, it sort of is," Leanne said. "It's your half birthday."

"It's exactly halfway between your fifth and sixth birthdays," Luther said. "Actually, I was looking for any excuse to fix up this bike and give it to you."

"But where am I going to ride it?"

"Oh, that's the other surprise. We're moving to Oregon. Papa's going to grow grapes."

"Does this mean I won't be going to school again?"

"No, but you wouldn't be going to school until late August or September anyhow. I'm sure you and Mama will find plenty to do this summer at our new home."

Another season, another reason to move. Apricots, cotton, lavender, and mint. When will we ever settle down? Papa loves green. As soon as he wins the battle of the blight or whatever else is bothering the orchard owner or farmer, we're moving again.

"Are you sure you want to do this, Luther," Leanne asked while Tori was in her room, changing out of her pajamas.

"I know it's hard on her, but all she really needs is consistency. It's not the configuration of the clapboard shack or trailer we're living in, it's us and her routine. We're her home. You can be her teacher again if it would make you feel better."

"It's not what would make *me* feel better, but what's good for her. I don't care if she's the smartest child in the whole school. I want her to be the happiest, most well-adjusted."

"Yes, me, too." Luther sighed and shook his head. "But how can she be happy and well-adjusted if we're miserable? I'm sorry, but I have to have a challenge. Anyone can earn a few bucks by pulling fruit off a tree."

"What makes you think that's all you do? Except for that mint-growing venture five years ago, every field you've touched has thrived. The only reason you're not making a decent wage is because you don't go blowing your own horn and let them know you have a doctorate. Or tell them about how you fine-tuned their fertilizer and irrigation schedules and that's why they have record-breaking harvests. I know no one is willing to pay for a horticulturist but mark my words, you let these landowners know that when you're on board, they're making a hell of a lot more with you than without you. They've been getting your college-level skills, even if you're job title is field supervisor."

Luther chuckled. "Yeah, who would have thought that my two years of high school Spanish would come in so handy, earning me my living where eight years of college couldn't."

"You're more than a translator who knows how to read labels and set up pest strips. Please, whatever you do in this next job, let them know who you really are. And for heavens sakes, ask for a decent wage! We need another vehicle. Our station wagon was worn out years ago!"

"Well, I'll see how it goes. I will ask them for a company truck, though. No more hauling fertilizers in the family rig!"

***

"Wow! It's so green!" Tori said. She rolled down the window and stuck her face into the wind. "And it smells so happy!"

"So, you really are your father's daughter," Leanne said with a chuckle.

"Of course, I am," Tori said. "Who else's would I be?"

"I mean, you take after him, not me, where it comes to plants and such. Who else would say that plants smell happy?"

"Well, they do. And marshes smell sad because they're rotting,

34

but composts piles smell young because they're transmuting from waste into energy, eager to help more plants grow."

"Now that poet aspect – weaving words not usually associated with each other, creating unusual but picturesque descriptions – that you get from me," Leanne said.

Tori kept facing out the window. This trip was taking forever! The roads went on and on and on, up and down, more twists than a bag of pretzels. And the hills were more like oversized gopher mounds.

"Do they have mountains in Oregon?"

Leanne turned around in her seat to face her. "Of course, they do. We've seen lots of them yesterday and today. These here are more like foothills but we saw lots of mountains around Redding."

"But they didn't shoot straight up and there was barely any snow."

"After we get settled, I'll take us for a day trip to Mount Hood. That's covered with snow all year round. Did you know you can even ski in the summer there?"

"But Hood's only one big bump, not a whole range like we saw when I was a baby."

"What? You couldn't possibly remember that!" Leanne said. "You were only two months old."

"Uh-huh," Tori said. "I remember it was really cold but you wanted me to see how tall the summits were. You bundled me up and held me close and told me that maybe one day, I could climb to the top of a mountain that high."

"You must have seen a photograph," Luther countered.

"Nuh-uh. I don't remember seeing any baby pictures of me. Ever!"

"She's right," Leanne said. "You had to sell our camera so we'd have enough money for gas to come across country. The first photos we had of her were spoiled when the water heater flooded."

"Well...well...I think you must have seen pictures of those

mountains in a book or magazine. There's no way a baby can remember what was going on when she's only two months old!"

"Yeah-huh," Tori said, then sat back in her seat, not wanting to try to convince him. *I remember everything!*

An hour later, Tori awoke from a nap, flinching at the realness of her dream.

Her two sisters were next to her but she could see them now, not just feel them bump and tumble over her. They had just been born, pulled out of their wet and warm world. She missed their touch but knew they were near. That had to be them squalling. They sounded just like her: angry that they were apart. She remembered the bright light and a new sensation: fabric. Then it was dark and they were all snuggled together again. Suddenly, wham! They were gone again and people were talking. It was cold, very cold, and then she was warm again. Mama had her but her sisters never came back.

Tori inhaled, recalling the first time she'd smelled her mother's scent. She'd figure out where her sisters were one of these days. She'd have to keep it to herself that she remembered them, though. Nobody understood or even wanted to try. Not Melinda, Mrs. Johnson, or even her parents.

She was certain that they had all been together once. She really did remember everything about being born. She wasn't imagining them, either. They were as real as she was.

"Oh, you're awake now. Did you have a good nap?" Leanne asked.

"Uh-huh. Hey, where we're going, do you think they'll have sidewalks so I can ride my bike?"

"No, but I'll show you what they do have when we get there. It'll be even better. Leanne, how much further do we have?"

Leanne looked at the odometer and then her note. "We just passed milepost 90. Our turnoff is just ahead. Oh, I'm so excited! Our very own vineyard to maintain."

"Why are there so many Christmas trees and why are they so

small?"

"They're small because they're baby trees," Luther said, " and there are so many because this is where they grow them for people all over the United States. Or one of the places they grow them."

"Wow… It'd take a lot of popcorn to make strings to decorate all of those!"

"Oh, right here!" Leanne said. "Take this road until it ends."

"If You Can Imagine Vineyards," Tori read. "That sounds like a fun place to work."

"I hope so. Let's go in and meet some new people."

The crew of three stepped out of the aging station wagon and stretched, taking in the vastness of the rolling hills that surrounded them and the newness of the modular office, so unlike the buildings or trailers Luther had worked before.

"I think I'm going to like it here," Tori said. "It looks like this place is just beginning, just getting started like we are. We can grow together, huh?"

"Like I said," Leanne bragged. "My little girl."

"Hey, there! You must be the Greene family," the tall handsome man walking toward them said, his hand held out in greeting.

Luther shook it heartily. "You don't look like a Julio Mendosa…"

"Julio had a family emergency and had to leave. If you're Luther Greene and are willing to take on extra responsibility right away, you have two sections of fertile Willamette Valley to turn into a vineyard. Oh, I'm Rick Rickman, by the way. I bought this property as an investment last year. I didn't think I'd wind up working it hands-on, though. Julio's a great guy, came highly recommended, but when your family needs you, you see to them first, right?"

"Yes, sir. I brought mine with me. This is my wife, Leanne, and our daughter, Tori Lynn."

"Beautiful women. Now, let's go inside and talk a little business first, then hop on the Gator and take a tour."

The vineyard owner noticed the look of terror on the young girl's face. "It's not an alligator, Tori Lynn," he explained. "It's like a mini car that goes up and down the rows. That way your daddy and I don't have to walk so much."

"You can call me Tori," she said, reaching out to shake his hand like she'd seen her father do. "And I think these paths are what Papa was talking about for my bicycle. Yes, he's right. These are much nicer than sidewalks. And softer to land on if I fall."

"Well, next week you might have a couple of young men here to ride with you. My son and nephew will be here for a few days before we leave for Europe. I planned to go there for pleasure, but now it looks like I'll be doing some research."

"*Vignobles et vignetos*? Luther asked.

"Yes, vineyards in France and Italy. If the weather is good, we'll also sail to Greece. They grow a *cabernet sauvignon* there that's supposed to be exquisite."

"If it's possible to bring back cuttings, I'd be interested in getting a few. I'm not sure what varieties you're growing, but I'd like to see about bringing in some heirlooms and hybridizing some new ones. The world can always use a few new fruits."

"Like pluots?" Tori asked.

"Yes, dear, like pluots."

"Looks like the next generation hybridizer is already taken an interest in your work," Rick said.

"She'd rather work with me than just about anything."

"Except read," Leanne said.

Luther nodded in agreement. "I'd say it's going to be tough to find a school for her, but I think we've already decided to try hybrid homeschooling. One or two days a week with a traditional school so she keeps up with her social skills and activities, then the rest of the time my wife will work with her. I'm afraid we taught her too much too soon."

"I had the same situation with my son, Rich. He's a bright boy.

If he's anything like your daughter, there's no keeping them back. He's only eleven and doing college calculus for fun."

***

"Do I have to go to school," Tori asked, trying not to beg but willing to if that's what it took to stay home.

"Yes, you do. We agreed that you'd go at least one day a week; more if you want to."

"Who's we?" Tori asked, scowling. "I don't remember talking about it."

"Your papa and I had the discussion. You were miserable half the time in kindergarten but the other half, you enjoyed yourself. You have to learn to get along with people your own age."

"But they're so boring."

"Then find something you and the others are both interested in. Maybe sports or crafts. Life isn't just about words and numbers. Not everyone in the world can read, you know."

"Why not? I could teach them instead of going to school…" Tori saw her mother's frown and realized she was trying to make a point, not looking for help with ending illiteracy. "Okay, fine. One day a week. But that doesn't mean I have to like it."

"Well, it sort of does. If you go into it expecting to be miserable, you probably will be. Look at it as a challenge. You don't have to make everyone your friend. How about you just try not to fall down or wet your pants on the first day of school."

"Mama! I haven't wet my pants since I was a year old!"

"You were ten months old," Leanne corrected.

"I know. I was there, remember? I just rounded up for convenience. All right, I'll try."

Chapter 5: The Teen Years

June 2009

"Mama, do you remember those boys we met the first year we moved here?"

"The ones who taught you had to ride your bike?"

"Yeah, whatever happened to them?"

"Oscar and Rich? I don't know. Your papa might know. He's the one who handles all the emails with Mr. Rickman. I wouldn't doubt that one of these days, Rich will take over his dad's businesses. I don't know about the younger one, the nephew. Oscar was always so quiet. I don't think I ever heard that boy say a word. Nice enough and had the sweetest smile, but it seemed like he always had something on his mind."

"Yeah, I know."

"Why did you ask? I haven't thought about them in years."

"Oh, nothing really. I just found this old sticker in one of my books. Oscar gave it to me." Tori held up a decal that looked like it had come out of a vending machine.

"Oh, that's cute. A pink unicorn."

"Yeah, he kind of grunted and handed it to me. He had football stickers all over his bike. I think he got this one by mistake and it was too girly for him."

"Oh, speaking of the Rickmans, Mr. Rickman is coming out today. Maybe he'll have his family with him."

"Tell them I said, 'Hi.' I have some stuff to do."

"Tori Lynn…"

"Really! I do. I um… I have to um…"

"I'm glad you're a lousy liar but very unhappy that you don't want to at least say hi. You're seventeen years old now. One of these days, you're going to have to go out in the real world and get a job. You'll have to talk to other people, make real conversations, and eventually get your own home. Who knows, you might even wind up getting married and having your own family."

"Ew! Mama! That's gross."

"What's gross? Working or having a family?"

"I'm not afraid of work. I'll just keep helping Papa and take over his job when he's ready to retire. But I don't want a boyfriend and I certainly don't want to make babies."

"We already had this talk. It may sound complicated, but when the time comes – and if you've found the right man – I can pretty much guarantee you're going to like it. Having a baby? Oh, I would so love to be a grandmother…"

"Maybe you can borrow one. That would be simpler for both of us."

Leanne huffed in defeat. "I'm sure glad I only have one of you."

Tori's eyes widened in surprise, a grin of providence growing into a devilish smirk. Mama had just given her the perfect opening to an adult discussion on what really happened to those sisters she knew she had, and why they were a secret. Just as she had gathered the courage to jump in on the subject, she noticed the window. A cloud of dust was rising among the otherwise green and beige striped landscaped. A groan escaped. Someone was coming up the road. The Rickmans were here.

"Are you okay?" Mama asked.

Tori clutched her lower belly and said, "I gotta go. I think it's that time of the month a little early." Before any more discussion could be held, she rushed out the side door, leaving her mother to deal with the big boss and any male kin he may have brought with him.

Two minutes later, two men walked in the front door of the office. "Looks like we got here just a little too late," Rick said. "Was that Tori that I saw leaving?"

"Oh, hi, Mr. Rickman. Yes, she had a minor emergency to attend to. This isn't Rich, is it?" Leanne asked, nodding to the scruffy-faced young man with hunched shoulders wearing a knit cap.

"Oh, no, no. This is Oscar. Rich is back east, attending university. Oscar here doesn't have the desire to go to brick and mortar schools. He's more of a hands-on kind of guy. Is your husband here? I need to talk to him about some business opportunities I think he might be interested in."

"I'll call him," Leanne said. She picked up the radio. "Luther, you have company in the office. Don't dawdle. Over."

"Got it. Roger and out," Luther said.

Before Leanne could offer the men a drink, Luther was in the office. "I was on my way here when I got the call. Oh, hello, Rick. This is Oscar, right?"

Oscar looked up briefly and grinned, then nodded in greeting.

Luther shook both men's hands. "What can I do for you gentlemen?"

Oscar's grin grew into a full smile. He was being included in the conversation. He might like working here. He wasn't invisible or worse – in the way.

Rick looked around the room to be sure, although he already knew it was just the four of them. "Everything's great with the numbers and photos you've been sharing. The wine from those new mega-producing grapes will be the rage once it ages for a while, plus everyone will be wanting the plants. So, let's get down to the reason for my visit. I have a business proposition for you."

"It doesn't entail moving, does it?" Luther asked, looking at Leanne to make sure she felt the same way. Her anxious frown confirmed that she did.

"No, no. Everything can be done from here. The laws are changing in a hurry. I know I was going to expand into those eighty acres I bought next door that used to be Christmas trees, but rather than grapes, I want to put up some greenhouses."

Luther's eyes flitted from Rick's to the young man beside him. Rick nodded that it was all right to speak freely. "If you're talking about getting into the cannabis game, I'm a few steps ahead of you.

Actually, almost forty years ahead of you. Come on. I have something I want to show you. Leanne, we'll be right back."

The three men rode in the Gator to a massive greenhouse that was not visible from the road. "When did that go up?" Rick asked.

"This is the research station you authorized four years ago. I didn't think you'd mind if I used a few feet of it for my own personal use."

Luther opened the door and waited for their reaction. "Wow!" Oscar and Rick both exclaimed.

Rick looked at Oscar, surprised that the very reserved and timid young man had spoken. He grinned with contentment. Yes, his nephew would love working here.

Impossible to miss were the twelve massive custom-built wooden barrels hosting a small forest of marijuana plants at the back of the greenhouse. The three men passed between the long, wire-topped tables loaded with containers of grape cuttings, an orderly array reminiscent of a log-cabin quilt, the leaves of the merlot and chardonnay grapes separated onto their own tables, further defined by the ages of the plants.

Rick was a vintner and interested in them, but he'd come back and see them later. "Those are the biggest marijuana plants I've ever seen," he said.

"Really?" Luther asked as he stood next to one of them, showing off that it was already six feet tall. "Because it's barely half-grown. It won't mature until September or October when the days get shorter. If this was a full-on greenhouse with the right kind of lights and in-floor heating, I could have these girls growing all winter long. Oh, and just for the record, these are legal plants. My wife and I both have medical marijuana cards."

Luther watched as young Oscar pulled a bottle of hand sanitizer out of his pocket and cleaned his hands. He barely heard what Rick was saying as he watched Oscar inspect the plants, lifting leaves, looking for problems.

"I'm sorry, Rick. I'm a little distracted. Is Oscar a botanist? He looks like he knows what he's doing."

"We were talking about kids being prodigies? Well, this kid loves to grow. He's positively obsessed with plants and what makes them sick or thrive. He was taking peanuts out of the bird feeder and growing them in pillow stuffing when he was four. His obsession was driving my sister nuts, but I saw him for what he is: a genius."

Luther followed Oscar, shadowing him as the young man took a pinch of soil and tasted it. "Not too salty, is it?" he asked.

Oscar shook his head, flicked off the dirt, then gave him a soil-stained thumbs up, grinning.

"So, how much did you plan on putting under cover? And do you have someone to take care of the paperwork? That's a whole other business, fitting into the government's guidelines, making sure we have the right documents and aren't growing too much."

"Got two former NORML lawyers setting it up right now. It's too late in the season to start only because we don't have enough greenhouses set up. That's one reason I have Oscar here. If you don't mind, I'd like him to be your go-to guy on the layout."

"It's not too late," Oscar said, his sultry voice startling the two men.

"Because..." Rick prompted.

"I can hire a crew and have the greenhouses up in a week. The NORML guys have licensed clone vendors ready to sell to us with a phone call. They told me if they got the go-ahead, they could have us licensed to grow in a week."

"A week to set up the buildings and a week to get the paperwork in place. Both could happen at the same time. Okay, Oscar, I'll make the call. Luther, I know you're the man in charge of this whole operation, but if you don't mind working with Oscar, I'd like him to take on the burden of getting the tents and plants in place." He spread his arms out, indicating the hundreds of young grape plants. "You already have quite a bit on your plate. Last year's crop was fantastic.

44

The vineyards are thriving under your care. I don't doubt this year will exceed last's. As always, if there's anything you need, just ask."

Oscar raised up his hand.

"Yes, son?" Rick asked.

"I'll need a place to stay, preferably on-site. I'm going to be putting in a lot of hours."

"Is it all right if he pulls in a travel trailer back here? I'm sure you already have all the hookups."

"Go for it," Luther said, his eyes bright at the idea of having a huge grow operation and an eager young man to help make it come together.

Rick reached in his pocket and took out his gold card. "This one's yours. Use it for everything you need, including a home on wheels. I have the feeling that this will just be the first phase of our new venture."

"I never thought I'd see the day," Luther said.

Rick chuckled. "Forty years ago at Woodstock – smoking weed in the open, too many of us to fear getting busted – and now running a legal grow operation."

"You were there, too?" Luther asked, eyes wide as he took in the youthful appearance of the handsome billionaire.

"I was only fifteen at the time but fiercely determined and not easily deterred. Even back then if I wanted something, I went for it. I was in New York visiting my granny and sneaked away that August night. She about had a heart attack when no one could find me for four days. When she did, she didn't stop scolding me until I was back on the plane to my parents in England, escorting me right to my seat. Phew! That woman could sear the hairs off my ears with her creative brow-beatings."

"I have to admit," Luther said, "I feel a lot better about it since it is legal. I have a daughter now. Once she came into our lives, a lot of things changed. Of course, we missed it, but when the laws changed and medical options popped up, we were right there. Old age isn't as painful with a little canna-relief."

Rick looked at the size of the plants and shook his head. "By the hearty growth of the plants you grow, I'd say you're getting a lot of canna-relief."

"No leaf for us," Luther said. "Only the buds. Yup, these are the good old days now."

Rick smacked him on the back in familiar agreement. "Amen to that."

Thunk-thunk!

Both men turned at the sound of the fans shutting off and then coming back on. "What's that?" Rick asked.

"Sounds to me like Oscar's checking out the electrical panel. I think we're going to need to buy a bigger generator, too. We won't need lights for a while, but we will need constant ventilation and water pumps. Before I go see if he needs some help, is there anything else you need from me?"

"How about a handshake. I cover all the costs and you get 10% of the net profits as your bonus. Even with Oscar here, you're going to be putting in more hours. I want to make it right."

"As long as you and your guys are taking care of all the reselling and all I have to do is grow and harvest, I'm down with that."

Rick reached out and the two shook hands traditionally, then did a fist-on-top-of fist exchange like the two inner hippies they both were.

A handshake agreement and the billionaire and the botanist both walked away happy, both of them getting a great deal.

***

Oscar glanced at the movement behind the corner of the greenhouse then continued with his calculations, not concerned about the noise. There weren't any large wild animals in this region that concerned him. Moles and skunks were more of a problem than coyotes and deer. At least with doors on the buildings, the larger mammals were less likely to gain access to the plants than the vermin.

Cougars might be a problem if they were spooked. His mind tumbled over and over, potential problems and what he could do about preventing them distracted him from his primary task: finding out what was needed to get four mammoth greenhouses erected and operational in seven days.

He took out his phone and checked for a signal. Damn! No service.

"It'll work down by the office," a shy female voice called out from the area he'd seen the disturbance.

He nodded and grunted, not verbalizing the word, "Thanks," but letting it be known he'd heard.

Oh, yeah! When I came out here ten, maybe twelve years ago, Luther had a little tow-headed daughter. She might be the one attached to that voice. Cute but crazy, jabbering on about how she was going to be the best bike rider in the world when she grew up. Shoot! She couldn't even stay on the path without me running along behind her, holding the bike seat to keep her upright.

Musing as he walked, his face down to watch for the bars to pop up on his phone indicating he was in a service area, Oscar almost walked into his uncle's SUV. He heard the tittering of someone laughing at his near collision.

Silly kid. He hit the icon and redialed his last call, then spun around suddenly to see if he could catch sight of her.

Not a kid! She's a grown woman now, or pretty darned close. Curvy in the right places, too.

Oscar watched as she sprinted through the opening between the rows of vines, graceful as a gazelle, disappearing over the rise. "Hello! Is anyone there?" asked the voice on the other end of his phone call.

"Huh? Oh, yes. Samson? Yes, yes, sorry about that. I got distracted. You know that big pie-in-the-sky quote you and I were talking about yesterday? How soon until you can have it ready to ship? You did? Really? Great! Here's the address. You can either bill

47

Rickman Vineyards LLC or I'll give you a credit card. Okay, send the invoice to the usual address. Yes, it's great to have a rich uncle but even better to have one who trusts your instincts. I don't think I forgot anything but one thing I'll need out here is a bigger generator. Do you think you can hook me up? Really? You're sure it's in good shape? Yup, 100KW would be just fine. Can you arrange delivery and payment on that, too? Fantastic. I gotta jet. It looks like I need to rent a few pieces of equipment to level and compact the foundations. The ground isn't as flat up close as it looks in photos. No, I won't be able to send you any of the harvest. If you want any, you'll have to come and get it yourself. And bring your medical marijuana card! We're not doing anything illegal here. It's all on the up and up. All right. I'll let you know if I need anything else. Oh, and text me the carrier and BOL number. Bye!"

Leanne heard an unfamiliar voice. She listened at the opened window. It had to be Oscar. For someone who didn't talk much face-to-face, the young man was sure chatty on the phone. She sat back at her desk and watched through the front window as he went to his uncle's Hummer to get something. He moved differently now, too. Just half an hour ago, he was shrunken down, timid as a scared dog. Now he was standing tall. Broad-shouldered and handsome despite that tacky knit cap and two-week-old beard. Better not let him get too near Tori when he was strutting like this! She may say she didn't want anything to do with guys, but this one was spewing appeal!

"Pfft! Less than an hour ago we were chatting about men and babies. How could I have been so eager for a grandchild? I'm not ready for my little girl to grow up! I'll have to make sure I keep those two apart."

Chapter 6: Forbidden Fruit

Later that day

"Tori, would you put together a salad for dinner? We have some leftover chicken. That chopped up with lettuce, tomatoes, cucumbers, and red onions should be enough. Oh, and you can split that loaf of French bread and spread garlic butter over it. If we use the toaster oven, it won't heat up the house."

"I thought we were having spaghetti for dinner."

"Too hot to boil noodles. Remind me and I'll have your father change out the propane tank on the grill. We can start cooking outside again. I didn't think it was going to get warm so early."

"Just wait a few days. The weather is sure to turn back to cool." Tori paused, her curiosity stronger than her timidness about men. "Hey, Mama, how come that one guy didn't go back with Mr. Rickman?" She although already knew the reason – she'd been eavesdropping while the men discussed their new business venture – but wanted to hear her mother's version.

"Your papa has a new partner of sorts. At least, young Oscar is going to take over the cannabis growing."

"There are only a dozen plants and they don't need much attention."

Leanne came up to Tori and stood a foot from her face. She knew Tori was just seeing if she'd tell her what she already knew. "You know more than I do about what's going on with the new venture. You were there, listening. I had to depend on your papa's memory to tell me everything. So, since that's the case, how long do they think it'll take to get this up and going?"

"A week," Tori said. She opened the refrigerator and started pulling out the components of the salad. "At least that's what Oscar said. I think that's nearly impossible, though. They plan on setting up greenhouses on that parcel over the hill that had all those Christmas trees on it. That ground is as lumpy as an old straw mattress: stumps and half-rotted trees, high spots and dried-up puddle ponds."

"Well, you can either work beside them and give them pertinent information, or you can work beside them and keep it to yourself, helping no one. Either way, you're working. Your papa did say he was a vested partner is this. Maybe this project will earn enough to send you to college."

"Ew! Why would I want to go to college? Anything I want to know, I can look up on the internet."

"Yeah, right. And those sources are so reliable. Darling, nothing will replace interaction and discussions with professors and like-minded people. Until you experience it, there's no way I can convince you, so I won't try."

Tori rolled her eyes, hearing the same lecture on learning. She took the knife out of the block and checked the blade for sharpness. Just to be sure it would cut through the tomato, she ran it across the steel a couple of times. "What we really need is some clearing equipment out here – like a brush or root rake or..." she said as she set to work on deboning and chopping the remains of the roasted chicken.

Tori felt her mother's hand between her shoulder blades. "Let the guys take care of it. If you see that there's an easier way to do it or a shortcut to save time, let them know. Until that happens, wait and see. Mr. Rickman seems to believe that Oscar can handle it."

"Okay," Tori said, ending the word on a high note, the doubt in her voice unmistakable. "But if they need help, I hope Papa asks me. I don't want them to think I'm a butt-insky know-it-all."

"There are only a few people involved in this project. If you approach them with a positive suggestion, they'll appreciate it." Leanne paused, thinking about the dynamic and often defiant attitude Tori approached every situation with. "Or at least they'll listen to you. Be gentle, though. Sometimes you have to sneak up on a puppy to give him a pill, not sit on him and cram it down his throat."

"Wouldn't know. I never had more than a goldfish," she said with a pout.

"Well, I am sorry about that. With your father's allergies, that's the best we could do."

Her knife held high so it was out of the way, Tori reached out and gave her mother a one-armed hug. "I know, Mama. And Papa also told me that it was you with the allergies, not him. He only claimed them so you wouldn't feel so bad about it. He'd rather have me angry at him than you. It's just part of life. I have so much freedom that not having a needy pet was probably the best for me."

Leanne smiled weakly and returned the hug. *But not giving you a pet to be responsible for was a huge mistake on our part. You would have been better off caring for a critter – learning to be responsible – while I dealt with cases of tissues and buckets of antihistamines!*

Twenty minutes later, Luther had arrived home, as chipper as if he'd just won five-hundred dollars on a lottery ticket. He set his broad-rimmed hat on the hook on the wall. "Well, this might work out great – having an extra set of hands and a young, strong back. It's going to take a while for that truck and trailer to get here. In the meantime, what's for dinner?"

"Chicken salad and as soon as you swap out propane tanks on the grill, garlic bread," Leanne said, setting the last plate on the table. "It's too hot for the toaster over, too."

"Consider it done," Luther said and put his hat back on. "Oh, and you might want to put some of that salad in a container and take it out to Oscar in the greenhouse. I guess I'll start calling that Number One since we're going to have at least five of them this year and more in the future. I doubt that he wants to take the time to go to town to eat. That young man's going to lose his voice if he's not careful. He's been on that phone of his non-stop since he got here."

"Oh, that's so sweet," Leanne said. "A young version of you: hardworking and dedicated."

Tori rolled her eyes at her mother's reminiscing. "I'll chop up a couple of carrots and apples to add to the mix and maybe throw in some raisins, too. Stretch it out a little."

"Sounds good to me," Luther said and was out the door.

***

"Ah, fresh bread and salad, the perfect summertime meal," Luther said, patting his belly as he sat back. "Tori, why don't you ride your bike up the hill and take that dinner out to Oscar? You haven't seen him in years, but he might remember you."

Tori looked back and forth between her parents. They had that dreamy-eyed look that they always got just before asking her to take a long ride. Yes, they wanted some of their 'quality alone-time' together. She'd rather be far away than hear the giggles behind their bedroom door, even worse when they tried to suppress them with a 'Shush, Tori will hear us' admonishment.

She wanted to face Oscar again as much as she wanted to smash her thumb with a hammer, but she'd figure a way to deliver the salad and bread without actually meeting him again. "How about if I take a long ride after? I can check on the pest traps while I'm out there?"

"Yes, I'd appreciate that. There's a high wind forecast for tomorrow. I want to make sure whatever insects were caught aren't blown out," Luther said, Leanne's hand on his, her smile growing at the promise of a late afternoon liaison.

"Don't worry about the dishes, dear," Leanne said. "I'll get them. Go ahead and pack up the rest of the garlic bread to go with that bowl of salad. Oh, and make sure you take a fork and a few napkins for him. I doubt he has any utensils."

"How about a tablecloth, candle, and bottle of wine, too?" Tori said, ending with a huff of sarcasm.

"Actually, that's a good idea," Luther said. "Maybe not the candles and wine, but all he has to eat on are the tables in the greenhouse. A dropcloth would be nice, as would a bottle of water. I don't think there are any cups out there."

"He can drink out of the hose like I do," Tori said, dropping the

52

salad into the cloth shopping bag.

"Tori Lynn Greene!" Leanne scolded. "Why are you so mean?"

"I'm sorry. I'm not used to having anyone around…"

"Well, get used to it. You're not going to live life as a hermit. You have too much to offer the world to be hiding in the garden or between rows of grapes."

"But I like plants more than people!"

"And how many people do you know? We made a big mistake, homeschooling you for most of the last eleven years. Starting this next semester, you're going back to public school."

"But Mama! I don't want to go!"

"Enjoy this summer and your solitude because come September, you'll be thrown into a pond of people, learning to swim in social circles, and get along with people with both the same and dissimilar interests," Leanne said.

Luther looked at his wife, shocked at her insistence but glad she finally was agreeing with him.

"Papa?" Tori asked, hoping he'd come to her defense as he always did.

"You're seventeen, Tori. You have to learn to interact with others one of these days. Consider this the big bandage you've put off removing for the last eleven years. You have to do it. We can't shelter you forever. What's going to happen when we're gone?"

"But…but…where are you going?"

Leanne scowled. "We're starting our sixties now, dear. When you're my age, I'll be over a hundred. Do you know what the odds are that anyone will live to be that old?"

Tori remained mute, frowning. She knew.

"Less than ten percent that I'll still be alive which means over ninety percent that I'll be dead. The statistics are even worse for your father since he's male and already older than I am. We don't want to leave you alone in this world, unable to interact with others. We know you're a bright, charming woman, but others don't. And they won't know because you freeze up or hide as soon as you see them!"

"Fine. I'll take this to Oscar. But I'm going to check all the bug traps, so don't expect me back for a long time."

"I expect you back home before dark," Luther said. "There's no way you can check them in the dark."

"I'll take a flashlight."

"You can take a flashlight, a candle or fifteen boxes of matches, but I still want you back before dark. Understand?"

"Yes, Papa."

Luther stood next to her and gave her a big hug. "Sweetheart, we love you. If we didn't, we wouldn't want to see you grow. Just consider meeting new people as hardening off a plant before putting it in the garden. By going to school for a year, you can get used to people gradually. Spend a few hours with them as you all work together on projects, and then come home to us. I'll have Oscar here to help me if it's something your mother and I can't handle."

Tori huffed but didn't reply.

"And as far as staying gone too long this evening, if something happens to you, I want to be able to find you. I know you're young and strong but life sometimes throws us a fastball."

"That's a curveball, but I know what you mean. All right."

Tori tossed the bread, utensils, large dish towel, and an empty cup in the bag and looked back at her parents, holding back the tears. They were kicking her out.

Luther saw her sniffing and knew it for what it was. "Sweetheart, you have nearly three months before school. Maybe you can start working with Oscar. You two got along great when you were little. From what I see, you both have the same interests, too. Just one year of high school is all we're asking. Who knows? Maybe you'll find something else that interests you and you'll want to go to college to pursue them."

"And leave you and Mama?"

"Live one moment at a time. Just take the dinner to Oscar. You can figure out the rest of life later."

"Okay. I'll try."

***

The door to the greenhouse was open. *Ergh! Doesn't he know that's just an invitation for whiteflies, aphids, and beetles to come in?*

Tori stepped in and looked around. If she had her druthers, she'd just drop the bag of food and split. But only five minutes earlier, she'd committed to trying to interact with people. A devilish grin sneaked in. *And if by interacting that means I get to chew out Oscar for leaving all the plants in the greenhouse vulnerable…*

She set the dinner on the table just inside and closed the door behind her. Then she saw it…or them. Two feet were sticking out under the table. She walked over slowly. Was he asleep?

A moan of discomfort came from his unconscious body followed by coughing as he awakened.

Tori squatted down near his feet and whispered, "Are you okay?"

His frustrated grunt as he shifted positions scared her upright. He sounded like a wild animal! She rushed back to the door, hand on the latch and ready to leave, then paused. What would she tell her parents? Shoot! She couldn't tell them anything. They were spending 'quality time' together and she didn't want to barge in on them during *that*!

"What happened?" he asked, his voice still low but no longer menacing.

"You turned into a werewolf," Tori said, then started giggling nervously.

"Huh?"

"Sorry. I say stupid stuff when I'm scared."

"Tori?"

"Uh-huh."

"You got big."

Tori glanced from his feet up toward his head, and then back at his very large sneakers. "So did you."

Oscar started to sit up, then collapsed back to the floor.

"You'd better stay put for a minute," she advised. "Let me get you something."

Quick! Think! What in the world could you get him that would help? Here you thought you were so smart, watching all those videos and reading all those books on emergency preparedness and you freeze up! Freeze, that's it. Give him a cool cloth to reduce swelling.

Tori grabbed the dishcloth from the food bag and quickly doused it with the hose, waiting just long enough for the water to run cool. She squeezed it out then dashed back to Oscar to try out her self-taught first aid skills.

He hadn't moved but was now flipped over, staring up at the bottom on the table above him, frowning.

"Here, put this wherever you clunked your head," she said and handed it to him.

He didn't take it from her or react to her presence. He was mesmerized, absorbed in whatever it was he was studying. Rather than ask, she leaned down and looked up at what he was focused on.

She stared up at what she thought was the same spot. "I don't get it," she said. "What's so interesting?"

He reached up and pointed to the intersection where the bottom of the table was welded to the top. "If they had attached it here instead, not only would it be stronger and have more clearance, but I wouldn't have hit my head."

"Okay, but what were you doing under the table?" Tori asked, staring at the same poor design.

"Picking up this," he said. He held out his fist and waited for her to hold out her hand.

Curious about what it was and surprised that she wasn't the least bit afraid of him, she opened her hand and accepted the token.

"My charm! I thought I'd lost it. Oh, thank you, thank you."

She heard him grunt and realized she was in his way and he couldn't get up. She scooted back. "Don't move too fast now…" she said, offering him help.

He looked at her offered hand, then rolled over onto his knees. "I'm too big for you," he grumbled and grasped the edge of the table to pull himself up.

Tori watched to make sure he wasn't going to fall over and when he was upright, she said, "The reason I'm here is I brought you dinner. We couldn't see that you had a way to get any for yourself since your uncle just dropped you off and left. I guess he figures you're going to sleep in the greenhouse, too."

A slight smile of irony tried to emerge, but the pain its movement caused stilled it. "Don't worry; I have a plan." He looked at her and saw she was intent on the metallic trinket in her hand and may or may not have heard him. "What is it – a comma?" he asked.

"It's a goldfish." She moved next to him and held it up so he didn't have to bend over to see it. "I've had a pet goldfish ever since I can remember. I'm trying to talk Papa into letting me have a whole bunch of them. If I could dig a big hole, I could make a pond. Papa says a pond would draw too many mosquitoes, though."

"Why not get a big container and set it in here? If mosquitoes come in, the goldfish would eat them. And the water would…"

"Be great for fertilizer, right?" Tori said, finishing his thought.

This time, Oscar worked through the discomfort and smiled. Someone who thought like he did!

"'Great minds think alike,' my papa says," Tori said. "I want a big container, though. I was thinking maybe an empty drum. But not one that once had oil or antifreeze or anything toxic like that in it."

"Why not get a watering tank – a trough – like the ones they use for livestock? It'd have to be plastic, though," Oscar said, his voice no longer soft, louder now that he had someone to share ideas with. "The zinc from the galvanized ones leach into the water. It'd kill the fish."

"And we can put a pump in it and use the fish poop water on the cannabis plants!" Tori said, hopping up and down, bouncing on the balls of her feet with excitement. "Better than that starting all over with hydroculture because we already have the plants half-grown. The fish will feed on the mosquito larvae, too. It's a win-win-win situation!"

"I can order the tank to be brought in with the other supplies." Oscar stood tall and looked around the greenhouse, calculating how much water would be needed for the twelve planters. "We won't be using the tank water exclusively for the pot plants. I mean, they need just regular water, too, so we don't burn the roots."

"Well, yeah! Duh!" Tori said. "But we'll have to ask Papa if he wants to use any on the grapes. Those are his babies."

"What kind are they?"

"They're some heirloom varieties he got started from cuttings your uncle brought back from Italy. They found some old, grown-over vineyards back in the hills somewhere on one of the islands. He sorta, kind of smuggled some canes and root cuttings out of the country. Don't tell anyone, though. I think it might be illegal."

"Nah, it's not illegal. He's on at least a dozen different boards in as many countries. They swap and trade all the time. I know about that one. Rumor is that the vines are from the days of Nero."

"Really?" Tori squeaked, fascinated. At hearing a new tone – giddiness – in her own voice, Tori suddenly shut down. "Oh, I brought you dinner," she said in a business-like manner, the spell of their planning for a future and reminiscing about the history of grapes broken by the sound of her own excitement.

Oscar looked around to see if someone else had come in and distracted her, then realized what it was. He felt it himself and reddened in embarrassment. They were attracted to each other. Maybe not on a major level, but the warmth and brightness of the mood was suddenly doused by the chilliness of their own fears at the emotional change. Better to focus on the project.

"Dinner?" Tori said.

"I'm sorry," Oscar replied, realizing he was off in his own world again and hadn't heard her. "Thanks. I think I'll start with two one-hundred-gallon tanks. Do you think you can find the goldfish or do you want me to look?"

"I can do that. I just buy feeder goldfish from the wholesale pet store. You have enough to do to get the greenhouses started. Oh, and by the way, I'm supposed to help you with that. The ground is dry now, but I know where all the low spots are on the old Christmas tree lot. And how are you going to put in a foundation and set up the structures in a week?"

"A construction crew and their equipment should be in here at daybreak," Oscar said with confidence.

"You'd better put your stakes up tonight then. They'll lose at least an hour of work time because of the morning fog. It gets so thick out here, they won't be able to see the corners."

"Dang! I knew I forgot something." Oscar bent to his phone, ready to call in and have them added to his order, then remembered he didn't have cell service.

"I can help with that," Tori said. "We have lots of marker stakes in the shed. Go ahead and eat. I'll be back before you finish the garlic bread."

Without waiting for his reply, Tori was out the door, eager to get out of his presence.

Or so she thought.

She had never felt lonely. Ever. At least since kindergarten. Her parents were always a bike ride away. Why did she suddenly feel so empty? She looked down at the front fender of her bicycle. Earlier today she had put on the unicorn sticker he had given her years ago, even before she knew he was coming. Was it some kind of omen?

"Stop being so dreamy, woman! You should never have picked up another one of Mama's novels. Stick to non-fiction! It's safer."

Tori dropped her bike at the front of the storage shed, punched in the keycode, and went inside, flipping on the light to scare away any spiders. There. The Gator was already empty. She backed it up to the

59

shelf loaded with wooden supplies and pulled out four bundles of stakes with fluorescent-orange painted tops. After Oscar was done with them, she could put them back. Besides, since Papa was a partner in this venture, he wouldn't mind sharing these. She momentarily thought of asking him for permission, then grimaced, thinking of what he and Mama were doing.

"Mama said I'd enjoy it if the right man came along. Maybe she's right..." She shook her head, trying to get out of that untapped emotional area. "Just take him the stakes and help him set them up."

Oscar was outside of the greenhouse waiting for her, munching on the last bit of garlic bread, when she drove up. "Since you know where we're going, why don't you drive."

He hopped in and sat next to her, his eyes forward. Suddenly self-conscious, he swiped the crumbs off his two-week-old beard. *Why are you worried about your appearance? You've never tried to impress anyone before. Ever!*

"Right over here is the low spot. It's hard to see because the ground is completely dry. You don't want water running into the greenhouse or undercutting the foundation," Tori said.

Oscar nodded in agreement. "If you were in charge of this, where would you set up?"

"Since this is going to eventually be a year-round operation, I'd set it up so the long side is going to be facing south. The prevailing wind is from the west but it's not too gusty because of the mountain effect. This way you can have the doors open and cool it off quicker in the summer. I'd go uphill as far as possible to catch as much winter sun and avoid puddling. See those rises? I'd work with them, not against them. But I'm not the boss."

"Neither am I, but you know this area better than I do. All right. Let's walk it out and then put up the stakes."

Oscar watched Tori as she walked in front of him, dawdling intentionally to catch the view of her bubble butt as she half-sprinted ahead of him, excited about the new project.

"And we really need to keep this spot open. I come out here sometimes to watch the sunset. At Spring equinox, is sets between those two hills and at the autumn one, between those two."

"Then I'll make sure I save this area. One of these days, you might want a home here," he said softly, then wondered why he had said that.

Tori had been intent on showing him the view and turned back to scowl at him at his words. "I'm not moving away," she said. "I have a home."

"You're not going to live with your parents forever, are you?"

"Why not?"

Oscar shook his head and sighed. "I'm sorry. I don't even know why we're talking about that kind of stuff. I'm just here to set up and help run the cannabis operation. I don't mean to get in anyone's way."

"I'm sorry, too. I'm a little sensitive. My parents are older. We were just having a talk about them not living forever. Do you know how hard that is for an only child to hear?"

"Even tougher to deal with," Oscar said under his breath, then looked up and said boldly, "You set the corners and if I don't agree after I start with the crew out here, I'll ask you about it. Do you have the time to help me?"

"I'm a millionaire when it comes to having time," Tori said, then remembered her parent's earlier admonishment. "At least until the bills come due in September."

"Bills in September?"

"I have to go to school."

Oscar raised his eyebrows. He never thought about it but just realized she was probably underage.

"But only until January third. After I'm eighteen, I don't think they can make me do *anything*!"

He shook his head and grinned.

"What's so funny?"

"There's always someone, somewhere, who will make – or try to

61

make – you do something they want you to do that you don't. Age doesn't make a difference. Come on. Let's see if we can get this done before sunset. I'll bet it goes down right about there, right?"

Tori walked over and stood under his pointing arm to see where he was pointing to. "If not right there, pretty darned close," she said. She suddenly realized how near she was to someone who wasn't her parent and ducked away.

Oscar stayed focused on the outside, not moving a muscle as she darted away from his side. It wasn't until she was gone that he realized that the warmth of her nearness – the same that he had felt in the greenhouse – had come and left again. Why her? Other people – even women he had crushed on and dated – never pulsed his personal space like she did, causing it to fill and empty so drastically she could be a pool of warm water.

He shivered. Or a hot springs. Was he trying to sabotage the major project ahead of him, fantasizing about someone who could never be his, to distract himself so he'd fail? Was this too much for him to undertake and his uncle had made a big mistake trusting him?

The thunk, thunk of Tori hammering in the stakes brought him out of his trance. She wasn't a vixen after his money or an adversary looking to take him or his family down. She was a hardworking young woman who loved her family. She was also a silly girl who loved goldfish, riding her bike, and exploring new ways to grow plants. *Enjoy having a friend. Listen to her. Do not get involved on a romantic level. Better to have her as an ally than an ex.*

Chapter 7: School Days

August 2009

The summer of Tori's seventeenth year went by quickly. Oscar followed her suggestions about orientation and where to set up the greenhouses, letting her help him every step of the way. Luther was very flattered that someone – besides himself – paid attention to his daughter's advice. Leanne was equally tickled that their bashful little girl was carrying on conversations with a real human being – not her imaginary friends. Tori was still timid around the subcontractors and inspectors, though, and mysteriously disappeared when they came to the site.

The attraction between the young couple was obvious but neither parent spoke of it, afraid to jinx it. Even after their workday was done, Tori spent time with the young cannabis specialist. Her parents could have set their clock by her after dinner disappearance. As the days got shorter, her vanishing act got earlier. Tori had a standing date, although they didn't dare refer to it as such. She'd help clean up the kitchen or putter around the house until a half-hour before sunset. "I'm going for a ride," she'd say, then be gone. They didn't worry. They knew where she was.

Oscar's travel trailer arrived the third day after he was on the job. He parked it on the ridge next to the greenhouses, right where Tori had said the perfect viewing spot for sunsets was. They worked elbow-to-elbow, or at least within six feet of each other, for ten hours a day. After work was done and she had spent dinner at home, she was still eager to go 'sundowning' with him. The two watched the sun set, discussing what they'd be working on the next day, or just sitting silently. Content.

In late August, the perfect melody hit a sour note. Oscar felt bad that he was the cause of it, but he couldn't help it.

"Luther, after the harvest, I need to go back and spend some time with my mother. I really think we need to do a little reverse construction on the greenhouses, too. We, meaning I, need to have in-floor heaters installed in the spring. I want to wait until the winter rains come and see the flow down the mountains first, though. Not that I don't trust Tori's layout for the buildings, but if we're going to pour concrete and invest in all the plumbing, hardware, and labor to get it in place, I want to make sure there isn't a natural wash she didn't remember."

"That might make her feel a little insulted," Luther said, "but I agree with you, one hundred percent. Just having buildings where there weren't any before could make a difference. It's better to skip a planting and not make money than invest in one and lose double the amount."

"All right. I'll draw up the plans and figure the bill of materials, but I won't order anything until February. As soon as the harvest is over, I'll move the tables out of three of the greenhouses and into one. We can finish the last one off until later. I've never spent a winter here, but I understand it's pretty wet."

"I've seen it go six months straight without a sunny day, every one rainy or misting. Great for growing trees, but it can take its toll on human emotions. Yes, definitely take a break and spend time with your mother. I'm sure she'll appreciate it. Remember Oscar, no matter how old you get, you're still her baby."

"I guess that's how you feel about Tori, too," Oscar said, then inhaled quickly, afraid that he was out of line.

Luther chuckled as his discomfort. He put his hand on the young man's shoulder. "She's our one and only. If we could have had more, we would have. I'm afraid we kept her too close, though. You're the only person she works with or even talks to. I don't know if she said anything to you or not, but we're insisting she go to school for at least a semester. Hopefully, she'll attend a full year, but I doubt it. She doesn't need the classes. She's already graduated high school, or rather, passed the tests." Luther laughed. "She did that right before her thirteen birthday just for kicks. Nah, she needs to be able to get along with other people."

"Oh, she'll be fine," Oscar said.

"Did you know she still talks to her imaginary friends?" Luther whispered. "She'd clobber me if she heard me tell you."

"I knew she did when she was a lot younger. If it gives her comfort, what difference does it make? She's great at what she does here. She says she wants to take over for you when you retire. Of course, she doesn't really want you to retire. She insists she's going to live with you for the rest of her life."

Luther canted his head toward his shoulder, looking at Oscar quizzically. "She talks that much to you?"

"We talk about everything. I even teased her about saving that little unicorn sticker I gave her when I was here that first summer."

"She said she found it in an old book."

"She said the same thing to me and I believe her. She said it was like an omen that her friend was coming back." Oscar beamed at sharing the story, glad to have someone to brag to; someone who really understood Tori. "Having her claim me as a friend is one of the greatest honors I could ever have."

Luther nodded, a smile of gratification rising. "Oh, you don't know how happy I am to hear that. Not that she's claimed you, but that you've claimed her."

"I didn't say that," Oscar said, blushing. "I said it was an honor to…" He sighed in resignation. "I guess it's no use denying it. Yes, I really like her. A lot. I'm almost afraid to leave after harvest. I'm afraid the magic will be gone. That when I come back, I'll just be the guy who works here."

"No more sunsetting?" Luther asked, one eyebrow up.

"Yeah, no more sunsetting," Oscar said with a full frown.

"I'll tell you a secret. If the magic is gone, it was never really there. It was only an illusion. If the magic was real, it will still be there, sunset or not. Time – especially just a few months – won't make a difference. You were gone the first time for what, ten or eleven years, and you still have a connection?"

"Yeah, but we were just kids."

"And as far as this old hippie goes, you're still just kids. Leanne and I have been together for over forty years and still have that zing. When it's there, it's there. That is, unless you intentionally try to kill it. All I ask is that you never be mean to her. Treat her as you would want someone to treat your daughter, and we'll all get along great."

"Wow! Words of wisdom I wish I had heard from my father," Oscar said.

Luther patted him on the back. "I guess that's why I'm in your life: to give them to you because your father couldn't."

Or wouldn't. Oscar patted Luther's back in the same friendly manner. "I guess I'll close up shop for the day." He looked up at the sky. "Sunset's coming in about twenty minutes. I don't want to miss it."

"Wouldn't think of keeping you from it. See you tomorrow. Oh, and if I were you, I wouldn't mention needing to leave until a day or two before you're gone. It's going to crush her. I'd rather have your last few weeks or days here with her in a good mood. You don't want to be around her in a sour one."

"Thanks for the heads up. No reason to upset her early."

***

Early-September 2009

"These harvest machines are so fast," Luther said after watching the demonstration video. "For our own use, we always do it all by hand."

"Twelve plants versus twelve hundred plants?" Oscar said, pointing to the forest of marijuana plants over ten feet tall in front of him. "I don't think we could hire enough people to process that much bud."

"Still, Leanne and I will trim our own plants, thank you very much. There's a certain joy in preparing it yourself."

"Understood," Oscar said. "I'll make sure when the crew shows up that they keep away from your greenhouse. I'm glad Rick subcontracted this out and neither of us has to deal with the harvest, packing, or distribution end of the operation. Growing is the fun part. It's so hard to believe that they can go from little four-inch clones to ten-foot monsters in only four months."

"Yeah, and I'm glad we kept them all in greenhouses! I was talking to old Mike Cooper down the road. He was growing his plants outside. Lo and behold, a mile away, some farmer decides to grow hemp plants. You know, for rope and fabric and stuff? Anyhow, they seeded it, of course; they didn't use clones. Over half the acreage came up male plants. And you know what happens when the males get older – poof! All their little hemp pollen went sailing off in the wind, makin' love to his female plants. Seeds! Oh, he was pissed! Ruined his whole crop. He made back some money but not all of it. Yes, planting under cover does more than protect the grapes from the taint of marijuana stink. It keeps the girls making bigger buds, sterile, and pure to variety."

"Oh, and speaking of girls, how did Tori do with her first day of school?" Oscar asked.

"I'll let you ask her," Luther replied, looking down at his watch. "It's getting close to sundown. She'll probably tell you anyhow, but she had a rough time. Not only was she the new kid, but she's so quiet, the other kids took it as she was stuck up. You and I both know she's not, but she does have a little attitude. Still, the teasing's already started. I'd like to go in and throttle those bullies. All that would do, though, is get me thrown in jail." He rolled his eyes and smiled, adding, "But it might be worth it."

"No, it wouldn't just be sending you to jail. It would kick you even higher up on Tori's hero chart. You're already her idol."

Luther blushed, then looked at his watch again. "You'd better get going. This is the highlight of her day."

Oscar chuckled. "Yeah, mine, too. You brought up a stellar

daughter." He turned off the lights in the office. "I'll see you in the morning."

"No, sooner," Luther said. "We told her to bring you back to the house for dinner tonight."

"Got it. And thanks."

***

When Oscar got to his trailer, Tori was already sitting on their blanket, straightening out the wrinkles so it looked perfect. "Nice day for sunset viewing," Oscar said as he approached so he didn't startle her.

She looked up and smiled, her eyes twinkling with excitement. "Every day is a good day for it."

"Okay," Oscar said. "Spill. Why is every day a good day for watching a sunset?"

"Well, for one thing, it means school's out."

"Oh, a bad day, huh?"

"Every day is going to be a bad day there. I feel like I'm serving a prison term. Only ninety-nine days and I'm done with my sentence."

Oscar frowned as he did some quick calculations. "I thought you had to go to school until you were eighteen."

"I do, but I'm not going to start a new semester. I'm only going until December 23rd, the day the semester ends. My birthday isn't until January third, so I get an eleven-day reprieve."

"Get out of jail early, eh?" Oscar asked with a chuckle. He turned away from watching the pending sunset and saw she was frowning at his remark. "What? School's rough for everyone."

"Really? Even you?"

"Duh! Especially me!"

"Why? You have it all."

"Me?" he asked, chuckling. "Okay, promise you won't laugh if I tell you about what I went through?" Tori's shrug of non-commitment was enough for him to continue. After his short talk with Luther, he didn't want to be right. He'd rather help her build up her own wall of protection from those creeps at school who teased or bullied her.

"I don't know how much you know about boys, but when they hit puberty, their voices change. It was just starting to change when I was here years ago. That's why I didn't talk much then."

Tori nodded but didn't comment, waiting for him to give a valid reason for why his school years could possibly be as bad as hers.

"It took years for the squeaks and croaks to stop. Maybe if I had talked more it wouldn't have taken forever, but it was a miserable five years."

"Five years?"

He nodded. "Finally, I was a sophomore in high school. I'd grown a foot over the summer and let my hair grow out. I kind of sort of, used to hide behind it. My mother always went on and on about how beautiful my eyes were. Her flattery flipped on me, though. The compliment became the reason to keep others from seeing their color."

"Emerald green," Tori said with an impish smirk. "I looked."

Oscar turned to her. "I'm not keeping anything from you, Tori," he said with sincerity, then amended his statement. "Except anything that might get me in trouble legally."

She canted her head to the side, wondering what he meant, then dropped the question before it came out when he began speaking again.

"Do you know how hard it is not to talk when you have to give an oral report? It's impossible. I either had to fail a class or speak up. Failure wasn't an option, so I spoke. My five-minute report on methods of cloning tender perennials became the subject of everyone's gossip."

"I think you sound like Gregory Peck. Dreamy."

"Yeah, that was the problem. They'd tease and taunt me until I talked, just so they'd hear my voice. The girls would giggle and the guys – most of them – would laugh.

"The other guys?"

69

"They'd giggle, too," he said.

"I don't understand."

Oscar rolled his eyes. "You don't need to. What about you? Do they tease you about anything or are they just obnoxious jerks in general?"

"'You won't talk because you're so pretty,' the girls say, practically snarling and hissing with their claws out. Shoot! Me? Pretty?"

"You are. I mean, it's genetics mostly: your bright sky-blue eyes, glistening blonde hair, flawless skin, fit body. Whether you sabotaged what you were born with by eating junk food and being a couch potato; or ate right and stayed active, you'd still have the foundation of perfection. I'm sorry. I'm rambling. It's true, though. You're inherently beautiful.

"However," Oscar continued, sitting up straight for his declaration, "I sincerely believe that true beauty shines from within. You could have been as bald as a cantaloupe, with close-set squinty eyes, and a hook nose that went to Jersey and back, and I'd still think you were pretty. It's that caring, sharing person inside who's so radiant. You could have messed up this – my first solo operation – by giving me incorrect intel, telling me the wrong location for the greenhouses, feeding me contacts for lousy subcontractors or withholding information. But you didn't. You brought me dinner, helped me feed, trim, and prune the plants, and even shared your plans for a modified aquaculture with me. Your inexpensive idea helped these plants thrive at a low cost while still maintaining their organic certification."

"Yeah, well, Mama always said 'Do unto others' and Papa said 'Karma's a bitch,' so I figured no matter which one of them was right, I'd better invest in at least a little of both philosophies."

"Works for me," Oscar said, venturing an arm around her shoulders.

Elated that she didn't flinch, he snuggled closer. "It's getting cold. Let's watch our sundown, and then go have dinner."

He felt her shoulders tense. "Your dad and I were talking before I got here; he invited me then. Hey, lookie there." He pulled her closer and pointed to a hawk circling the vineyard below. "Rodent control."

Tori relaxed at his switch in topics. "Yeah," she said, burrowing as close as she could into his warm, solid frame, barely noticing the bird. *I could stay here forever!*

***

The next morning

"Do I have to go to school, Mama?"

Leanne held up two different colored flannel shirts for her to choose from. "What do you think I'm going to say?"

Tori scowled in reply.

"You told us you'd give it at least a semester. The semester ends December twenty-third and so you have…" Mama paused, trying to remember how long she had.

"Too long," Tori answered and swung her legs out of bed. "I don't think I'll ever agree to anything ever again."

"Never say never," Leanne said, setting both shirts on the dresser. "Hurry up or you'll be eating cold oatmeal in the truck on the way into school."

Tori growled as she set about her morning routine, rebraiding her two-foot-long braids that were fuzzy from sleeping in them. Even if she didn't want to go, she didn't want to look like a slob. She looked down at her feet, wiggling her sock-covered toes. "Easy decision. If I'm going to be miserable everywhere else, at least my feet can be comfortable." She put away the new mary janes her mother had set out for her and put on her well-worn cross-trainers.

"Easier to walk home in these if things don't work out," she huffed, then started day two of her sentence.

No one had paid much attention to her or her rural appearance on the first day of school. The chatter and jeers were directed at others, friends and classmates they hadn't seen all summer, catching up on brags and gossip. She waded through the nonsense, finding her way to the lab and art classes her parents insisted would benefit her the most.

The only reason she made it through that first day without leaving was she knew that Oscar would be upset if she left. She knew he was proud of her for working through her discomfort, glad that she was at least giving it a try. After dinner, he had given her a quick squeeze of reassurance across the shoulders. Oh, how she wished he was brave enough for a face-to-face hug. Her shoulders hunched up in anticipation. Or maybe even a kiss.

"I promise you'll survive this," he said.

"And then what? Surviving isn't living."

"Well, it certainly isn't dying, either." Oscar saw she was near tears. She had hoped for reassurance, not her friend agreeing with her parents.

"Look, consider this a storm you have to get through. You're young and able to bend with the gusts of rudeness and adversity. You may not realize it now, but this is making you a stronger person," he said, "giving you deeper roots."

Sniff. Sniff.

Oscar knew she was too upset to speak. "Hey, I'll help you in every way I can. Deal?"

"Deal."

***

"Another day, another drama," Tori said to her image in the mirror. "At least I have sundowns with Oscar to look forward to."

She walked into the kitchen, her chin out rather than hanging down in depression.

"Well, you seem like you're in a better mood today," Mama said.

"We have a lab this morning that interests me," Tori said casually, using that as an excuse. The last thing she wanted to admit to anyone was that she had been hugged by Oscar yesterday and was looking for more of the same. Or maybe something even better.

Tori picked up a piece of toast and set it on her plate, then grabbed the jar of apple butter. "I know the principle behind growing crystals, but the lab has more raw materials than we ever had when we did it when I was homeschooled."

"I'm glad you could find a bright spot to focus on," Papa said, setting down the newspaper. He suspected the real reason was just to pass the hours until she could spend time with Oscar. Now that the professional crew was taking care of harvesting the plants, there wasn't much – other than paperwork – to do.

***

The teacher explained in detail what the project was: growing crystals. She held up a bottle of bluing. "Many of you may have grown crystals on coal or charcoal with bluing, ammonia, and salt. We're going to start a project using bismuth, a heavy metal, today."

Tori tried to hear the teacher, but the three others at her table were chattering about their plans for the weekend. "Shush," Tori said.

All three at her table plus the students nearby immediately quieted and stared at her.

And then started laughing.

Tori wanted to cry but didn't. "How can you hear what the teacher's saying if you're talking about who's buying the booze for the punch?" she hissed, staring at the broad-shouldered boy in the football jersey in front of her.

He paled as he looked up at the teacher. "It wasn't me," he said.

"It better not be," the teacher said, her eyes narrowed. "One more mess up, mister, and you're off the team."

"Ooh-ooh!" The class chanted, laughing at him.

He turned and scowled at Tori. "You're dead meat, Blondie."

Tori flipped her braid over her shoulder and looked at the teacher. "As you were saying?"

The teacher grinned at the precocious new student, then began anew, speaking louder, taking courage from the girl who had dared put down the star quarterback. "We're doing two trays of crystals per

73

table. One dish will be fast-growing, the other slow. The instructions are on your worksheets. Make sure you don't get the bluing on your clothes or body. It won't scrub off."

The students began their work, shuffling papers and measuring. Tori was intent on arranging the bismuth in the pan and didn't feel Jackson the quarterback lift up her braid. Nor was she aware of him squirting bluing on it. It wasn't until she heard the stifled giggles of those around her that she looked up and felt the resistance on her head, his hand still holding her hair.

"Your braids are so beautiful," Jackson crooned, then laughed out loud, waving the end of her plait in front of her face, showing off its new intense blue color that ran halfway to her head, then he dropped it.

Tori glared at him, her teeth set, holding back the urge to bite the smirk off his face. Instead, she caught sight of the scissors on the middle of the table. "Really?" she asked, her narrowed eyebrows separating, one lifted up with impending mischief. "You really like my hair?"

"Yeah. It's such a gorgeous shade of blue," he said, laughing even louder.

Tori grabbed the scissors like a knife and pointed them at him menacingly.

Jackson took pensive steps backward, his shoes squeaking on the hard tile floor. He stumbled into a stool and kicked it aside, nearly falling down, catching himself at the last moment with one blue hand grasping the windowsill. He was cornered by the crazy new kid, pinned down by the scissors in her hand.

Tori reached up and made a show of putting her fingers through the handles, grandstanding as she tested them, snipping the air. The whole class gasped as one.

Jackson clutched both hands in front of his crotch protectively. *She wouldn't, would she?*

Turning the shears toward herself, Tori grasped her blue braid with her free hand, and with three angry snips, cut it off just below her ear lobe. She dropped the scissors on the table with a clang, then took one step toward Jackson, paralyzing him. Emboldened by his fear, she slapped the bluing end of her plait across his face, letting go of it at the last moment, dropping it in disgust.

The plait now rested on his shoulder, limp, staining his team jersey, his face painted with a long blue splash.

"There! If you like it so much, you can have it!"

Tori snapped up her backpack from the floor and walked up to the teacher. "I don't think I'll be coming back. The conditions here aren't conducive to learning. And yes, he volunteered to bring vodka to the party. He already bought it and it's in the trunk of his Volvo."

"Wuh...wuh... Well, bye," the teacher said, stunned. Her wide-eyed stare quickly turned into a grin of delight. She looked over at Jackson. Three young women and his male minion were tending to him, trying to wipe the Prussian blue dye from his face. "You are so busted, mister," the teacher said.

Tori listened outside the door, out of sight but within earshot. It was a miserable but memorable day. She strutted out the front door of the high school, glad that she had worn her walking shoes. It would take over an hour to walk home but she'd do it. No matter what she had promised, she wouldn't be coming back to *this* school!

She got to the head of the road just after noon. Hoping no one was watching, she walked through the vineyard, keeping on the service roads, bypassing the main road to the office, heading right to the greenhouses. Sooner or later, though, she'd have to let her parents know they didn't need to pick her up after school, today or any day.

"You're back early," her mother said.

"What are you doing here?" Tori asked, startled that her mother was in her sanctuary, not the office.

"I should ask you the same thing," Leanne said, then stepped closer, checking out her daughter's lopsided hairdo. "What happened?"

Tori sniffed, hoping to find some backbone, but it was futile. She was tired from the long walk, weak from missing lunch. Five miles was a long trek when you're used to biking everywhere. "I was attacked," Tori said, glad that she had found a dynamic word.

"Someone cut your hair?"

"Duh!" Tori said, not wanting to explain that she had done it.

"I'm going to call that school right now," Leanne said, her face brilliant red with anger.

"They already called me," Luther said, walking in on the pair.

"Why didn't you tell me!" she asked, her rage redirected at her husband.

"And where is your radio, wife?"

"Oh, shoot!" Leanne patted her pockets. "Sorry. Again."

Luther let the perpetual argument about keeping in communication drop and instead focused on his daughter. "Are you all right?" he asked Tori, pushing the wayward hair from her unbound partial braid out of her face. "Looks like Mama needs to even things up a bit."

Tori started giggling at his reaction but it soon turned into tears. "It was horrible!" she said. "They hate me! I didn't do anything, but they still hate me! How do they get away with it? Why?"

"Their parents don't care," her father explained. "I know that's not fair to the other students, but that's pretty much what it boils down to. Their folks shove them out the door, put dollars in their pockets, and ignore them so they can get on with their own lives. Years ago, folks needed their family. They worked together, ate together, helped each other with everything. Nowadays, Mom and Dad – if there are two parents – go to work, drop the kid off at school, and expect the teachers to take care of manners, respect, reading, math, everything."

"Yeah," Tori said. "And the students outnumber the teachers by so many, it's ridiculous."

"Hold on a minute," Leanne said. "I think I'm missing something in this discussion. What went on?"

"Oops!" Oscar said, walking in on what was obviously a serious family discussion. "I just need to pop in here a minute. I forgot my gloves."

"Go ahead and take a break," Luther said. "You might want to sit in on this. You're practically family. It's better if you hear it now so Tori doesn't have to tell the story more than once."

"Did the school call you?" Tori asked.

Luther looked down his nose at her, not even bothering with words.

"Oh, yeah. I guess they would need to call you if I left campus, huh?"

"Go ahead, sweetheart," Leanne said to Tori, nudging Luther at the same time to urge him to let up on 'the look.'

Tori closed her eyes and recited the story without emotion – as if she was reading a list of names from a telephone book. At least it was drama-free until she got to the conclusion.

"But at the end, it was the neatest thing!" she exclaimed, her face now radiant with elation. "When I got to that class, the teacher was so cowed by the students, it was pathetic. After I scared that full-of-himself jock to the point that he almost peed himself, the teacher found her voice. She wasn't going to take his snarky attitude anymore. I'll bet the same's going to happen for everyone else in that class, too. So, you know what? I made a difference. It felt so great!"

"Well, that's what we were hoping for," Luther said proudly, then took his tone down to humility level. "Sort of. We were hoping you would feel empowered in some way, but if you feel better about yourself for helping another person feel self-assured, that's just as good."

"Even better," Leanne said. "Two for one."

"And in only two days," Oscar added, grinning in pride at the girl he was so fond of. "Oops. Sorry. Not my place."

Luther said, "Nah, speak freely." He clapped the blushing young man on the shoulder. "Yup, that's my girl. What would take anyone else a year, she can figure out in two days."

Leanne spoke up, breaking the spell. "All right, everyone. Lunch might be a little late. I have to give my baby her first major haircut. When you decided to grow your hair out forever in kindergarten, I was wondering how long that would last. Well, at least, I have one long braid to keep in my treasure box."

"Yeah, you don't want that other one," Tori said with a devilish smile. "Dyed blue and covered with brat cooties."

***

Leanne used the step stool to reach the old wooden box, taking it down from the top shelf in her closet. "I haven't looked in this thing since before we moved here. I always meant to, but with moving and starting a new job, I either never had the time or I didn't remember. Come on, sit down with me. Who knows what treasures we'll find."

Tori sat beside her mother at the kitchen table, offering her a dishtowel to wipe off the layer of dirt and grime that had accumulated over the years with vineyard dust that seemed to sneak in through every window and door.

She watched her mother wordlessly, wishing they could get on with the exploring so she could get her haircut and dash back to Oscar. Even if there was nothing to do, there were always garden pots to wash and sanitize.

"There it is!" Mama screeched in joy. "Your father's old wallet. We used to hide a fifty-dollar bill in it. It was our emergency money. We came across the country when you were so little, poor as church crickets."

"Church mice," Tori corrected.

"Mice, crickets: what difference does it make? None of them have money. We always found a way to earn enough to get us further on down the road."

"How come you were so poor? Papa got his doctorate years ago."

"I guess you're old enough to know. We don't like to bad mouth people, but your father was a partner in a research company. He developed a new formula to treat clones so they'd root within in hours, not days. He was going to file for the patent in the morning, assured of millions of dollars from the horticulture industry. However, his partner printed out the research data and deleted all references to the project on their computers, saving it on his own laptop, then took the first train to the patent office. He filed for it under his own name, leaving your father out of all potential earnings. When your papa protested, the man got a lawyer and, long story short, we were left with nothing but our savings. If we had continued the fight, we may or may not have won."

Leanne glanced up at Tori, wanting to tell her that rather than hire a lawyer, they used all their savings and sold or pawned everything of value to buy her adoption. Their daughter was worth it, but there was no way she could share that secret.

"You and Papa really did go to Woodstock?" she asked, holding up the creased and faded tickets that looked genuine.

"Oh, my! It's still in there," Leanne said, glad to be distracted from her guilt. "Yes, we went when we were practically teenagers. I mean, I was, your father's older. Yup, we're serious when we say we're just a couple of old pot-growing hippies."

"Here's your same fifty-bucks," Tori said. "Money looked different back then."

"Yes, it did. What else is in there?"

Tori took the old-style fifty out to show her mother and found something behind it.

A laminated photo. Tori stared at it. Speechless.

"What is it, honey? You looked like you just saw a ghost."

She handed it to her mother, still stunned.

"Oh, that's so fantastic!" Leanne gushed. "And here we thought we didn't have any baby pictures left of you after the flood ruined everything. This was your father's favorite picture and it's even more priceless now."

Tori took the picture from her mother and studied it, making sure it wasn't modified or a mock-up. Nope. It was the genuine article. Her mother was nursing her. She didn't know much about babies, but she didn't look very old. She was round and chubby-cheeked, not gaunt and lanky like a newborn. Definitely too small to walk, too. *I really am their child. Then who are those other two girls I see? I could have sworn I had sisters!*

Tori felt her mother gently replait her remaining braid. "Are you all right, sweetheart?"

"Yeah, Mama. I'm just having a very emotional day."

Her mother kissed the top of her head, reassuring her. "It'll be all right. Trust me."

"Sure," she sighed. *The other kids were right. I really am crazy!*

Chapter 8: Hat for a haircut

Tori picked up the hand mirror, verifying both sides of her hair were even in length. She huffed in frustration. She'd worn braids ever since her hair was long enough to plait. Suddenly, she looked older. Was it the empowerment she had earned at school today or simply the change of hairstyle?

"I said, do you like it? I can cut off more if you want?"

"No, Mama. This is fine. If you don't mind, can I skip lunch with everyone? I'm tired after the long walk."

"And all the excitement?" Leanne prompted.

"Yeah, that, too," Tori agreed. She set down the looking glass. She wasn't even curious if she'd still see her two sisters if she looked into the bathroom mirror with it. Were they really just her imagination?

"Honey, this is part of growing up. You experienced at least one new and intense emotion today. Rage wasn't new, I know, but rage in defense of self is different than being mad at a person or situation. You also helped someone find her own power. That's a joy not everyone gets to feel, at least until you watch your child grow up and stand on her own two feet."

"Like you today with me?"

"Yes, I got that same joy today. Your father did, too," Leanne said dreamily.

Tori looked up and saw the sly smile Mama always got when she was feeling frisky about Papa. A nap now would definitely be a good idea. She'd need to take another long walk tonight so she was out of the house this evening. Or maybe she'd stay longer with Oscar after sunsetting.

"I'm going to take a shower before my nap, so please don't do dishes or laundry until I'm done."

"Got it. No hot or cold water surprises," Leanne said.

Tori stepped into the warm shower, the silkiness of the water on her skin different now that her hair wasn't interrupting the sensation. No covering over her neck or back. Or her breasts. She squirted a big blob of shampoo into her hand, realized she probably didn't need as much, then went ahead and used the full amount. It produced way too many suds; tiny dense bubbles that meant she definitely didn't need to wash it twice. She grabbed her washcloth and hurriedly soaped it up, not wanting to indulge in giving herself a shower smile. Frustrated with herself and life in general, she scrubbed hard, trying to wash away anger and humiliation, rushing through her usual routine, eager for the oblivion that sleep offered.

She dried off quickly, wrapped the towel around her head, then slipped into bed, naked and exhausted. Why was growing up so hard? Couldn't she stay a kid forever? "Silly ass! Nobody wants to deal with negative emotions! Stop thinking you're so special that you can skip over the pain and humiliation of growing up!"

Tori's last thoughts before she fell asleep were of watching a sunset with Oscar. No, she really didn't want to stay a child. She wanted to grow up and be a wife. But that didn't mean she didn't wish she could just skip through the rough times.

The sound of a gentle rapping at her door awoke Tori. "Are you all right, sweetheart?" her mother asked.

"Huh? What time is it?"

"Almost six. You've been asleep for almost three hours."

"Oh, shoot! Thanks, Mama. I'll be out in a few minutes. I guess I was more tired than I thought."

Tori shook her towel the rest of the way off her head, slipped on her sports bra and tank top, stepped into her sweatpants, and grabbed a flannel shirt to ward off the evening chill, tying it around her waist.

"What happened to you?" her father asked when she came into the living room.

"What do you mean?"

"You look like Medusa."

Tori stepped in front of the decorative mirror above the fireplace and groaned. "I forgot about my hair. I guess I'll have to do something with it."

"At least comb it," Luther said. He saw her frustration and added, "Don't worry. It'll come back. I promise."

"Just like everything else that's been happening to me, I want it to just hurry up and be over!" Tori took another look at herself, grunted, then went back to the bathroom to try to tame her hair.

It was impossible. The blonde tresses, so used to being contained in braids and weighted by length, were free and flyaway; clean, carefree, and full of static. She ran her comb under the faucet, wetting it repeatedly before swiping it through her slept-in kinks and curves, wild from being wrapped in a towel for three hours. She considered wetting it completely again but decided against it. She'd have to settle for the tamed-down mess rather than spend the evening with a chilled, wet head.

By the time she was done with dinner, she had forgotten about her new hairdo. Mama was still making googly eyes at Papa. Were they getting younger as she got older? Nah. Mama had shared the contents of Papa's old wallet with him before they sat down to eat. They were thinking of Woodstock and nursing babies. Ugh! A quick assist with washing dishes and she was ready to leave.

"I guess I don't have to ask where you're going," Papa said.

"Yes, we're going to watch the sunset. After that," Tori glanced at the shelf of DVDs and pulled one out without looking at it, "we're going to watch a movie."

"Sleepless in Seattle?" Mama asked.

"Sure, why not? It's one of your favorites, right? I guess I'll finally find out what all the hoopla's about."

Luther started to ask her not to stay out too late, then changed his mind. He glanced at the clock and did some quick calculations. An hour until sundown and then a two-hour movie. Tonight he'd bring out a bottle of wine, too.

Leanne walked over to Luther at the screen door, standing beside him as he watched Tori set the movie in the basket, ready to pedal up the hill to Oscar's spot. Oscar and Tori's spot. "It's a good thing I trust him," Luther said.

"She may not have been interested in boys before he came along, but she sure is now," Leanne added.

"He's a man," Luther said. "On the one hand, that's scarier. On the other, not so much. She's almost eighteen. One of these days, she's going to want to move away and start her own family."

"True, but she'll always be our baby. Come on, I hear that bottle of wine you've been saving for a special day calling us."

"You read my mind, wife," Luther said and kissed her on the temple.

***

Tori arrived at Oscar's trailer, excited for the sunset to begin. She rapped on the door then heard him holler at her. He was already up the hill, their blanket spread out, two glasses of lemonade set on the small side table they used for picnics.

"The low clouds and smoke from slash burns should make for spectacular colors tonight," he said, doing his best not to stare at her wild hair.

Too late. His gaze had lingered a moment too long. Tori's hand went up to her head. "Oh, man! I totally forgot about it!" she said, her eyes red as tears began.

"Here," Oscar said, taking off his knit cap. "This will keep it out of your eyes. It'll grow back. I promise."

"You sound like my father."

"I hope that's a good thing for you because I consider it a compliment. He's a cool guy."

Tori swiped the back of her hand under her nose, checking for nasal leakage. Assured that only a dribble of tears had made it out, she tucked her wayward locks under his hat. "Hey, this feels good. It's like my head is getting a hug."

"Yeah. Now you know why I wear it all the time."

84

"And here I thought you had premature balding," Tori teased. She looked up. "Hey, look. It's starting early. Let's time it."

Oscar started to offer her a drink then saw she was settling in. Yes, he'd rather cuddle up to her and watch a long sunset than sip on lemonade and munch on veggies. After a few minutes, he reached up and pulled up an edge of the knit cap.

"Don't. I have Dumbo ears," she said, her shoulder shrinking away from him, breaking their magic bubble of contact.

"No, you have magic elfin ears."

"You mean like I'm a magic elf or the ears themselves are elfin?" she asked, then laughed, knowing which one he meant.

Oscar leaned forward and held her face, turning her head gently to kiss each bared ear. "Lovely ears on a beautiful woman who is magical."

"Huh? I mean, I heard you but how am I magical?"

"You make my heart sing. Every muscle in my body and breath I take is charged with happy tingles when you're near me. The mere thought of you excites the cells in my body."

"Cells can't be happy," she protested.

He kissed her on the mouth without warning, quickly before he lost his nerve. "Did that make your mouth happy?" he asked. "Because if it didn't, I'll never do it again."

Tori replied by leaning into him, knocking him back onto the picnic blanket, returning his tentative buss with a full body contact kiss, breastbone to breastbone, her hands on his shoulders pinning him down. Absorbed in the moment and driven by instincts, her mouth explored his with abandon and he responded the same way.

Hormone-enhanced emotional reactions took over as their bodies ground against each other passionately, seeking more physical joining, stymied by cotton and zippers.

Tori shifted, trying to get closer to him. "Whoa, whoa, whoa," Oscar pled breathlessly, breaking away as she changed positions. "I mean, I'd like to keep going, but if we do, I'm afraid I won't be able to stop."

"Stop? Am I doing something wrong?"

"No, you're doing everything right. Too right..."

Ring! Ring! Ring!

"What's that?" Tori asked, embarrassed as she realized how brazen she had been. She felt her face redden and was glad that something had interrupted them. Hopefully, she would have time to think of an excuse for her bold response to his gentle kiss.

Oscar stared at his phone, the obvious source of the alert. "Danged if I know why it's ringing. We don't have cell service out here." He picked it up and saw his cousin's face on the screen.

"Hold that thought," he said to Tori with a grin of chagrin, then clicked answer on the phone.

"Hey, there, Oscar," Rich said. "I hope I'm not interrupting anything. I've been trying to call you all day. I remembered you said you didn't have cell towers out there, but I was hoping you had internet. Cool, eh? A long-distance call over wi-fi."

"Yeah," Oscar replied, answering the second question and also the first one about interrupting at the same time. "So, what's so important? I haven't heard from you in ages."

"Dad wanted me to get in touch with you. He's on a trip to Antarctica and in and out of service. He asked me to contact you about your mother. Have you heard from her lately?"

"Um, no. That's not unusual, though. We only talk around the holidays, and even then it's iffy."

Before Rich could reply, he held up his hand, asking Oscar to hold on. "I'm on the phone, sweetie. I'll be there in a few."

Oscar's eyes widened. It was Tori! Tori was standing behind his cousin, chatting about a dinner or something. He looked back and saw Tori was still on the blanket, sipping on a lemonade, letting him finish his phone call without interruption. "Who's that?" he asked.

"Oh, that's my girlfriend. I'm pretty sure we'll get married," Rich whispered into the phone when her back was turned. "I can't make it official until she's eighteen, though. She's a cutie, huh?"

"Yeah, huh."

"Oh, and about your mother… Dad said he talked to her just before he went into that dead zone. She's acting, how should I say…"

"Squirrelly?" Oscar offered.

"Yeah, that's it. Anyhow, it's that time of year again and he's worried she might do something stupid. He said damn the crops and harvest; would you go help her? She's his only sister and he can't get to her soon enough or he'd go. I'm sure he doesn't want you to mess everything up this first season, though. Are you at a point where you can break away and spend some time with her? I know things are a little uncomfortable with the two of you, but give her a week or two of your time. Autumn in Paris is awesome."

"You don't have to say anymore. I'll give her a call in the morning and see how she's doing. Oh, and congratulations on the engagement."

"Shush," Rich said, his smile growing. "Not yet. I'll tell you a secret, though. When you find the right one, it feels so perfect. It's like putting on your favorite shoes: comfortable and ready for a long journey."

"I'm not a pair of old tennis shoes," Vickie called from the background. "Hope to meet you one of these days," she said, walking up close to cuddle into Rich, both of them waving goodbye.

"Yeah, you, too," Oscar said, leaning closer, wishing he had a way to capture a screenshot and show Luther that Tori had a doppelganger.

The screen went blank but not before Oscar had noticed that there was a difference between Rich's girl and Tori: the ears. His gals ears didn't stick out. *Still, almost twins.*

"After the sun goes down, do you want to watch a movie with me?" Tori asked, letting him know that she knew he was done with the call.

"Yeah, sure." He looked at her and smiled. Worn but comfortable shoes. Nah, she was more like a worn and comfortable flannel shirt, ready for him to wear as they tackled the world together. He felt his excitement return and rolled sideways so it wasn't so noticeable. "Um, one thing, though. Normally I wouldn't mind, but I think we'd better stay away from romances and chick flicks tonight. I'd hate to get carried away and do something your father would have me arrested for. You're still only seventeen."

She looked away from him, hiding her scarlet blush. The sun was still a minute or two away from setting completely. "All right. But can we at least snuggle until the color is gone from the sky?"

"Hmm. How about until the first star comes out," he said, wanting a moment or two longer.

"Real star, not a planet," Tori amended, setting her lemonade back on the table. "Come on. The show's still on."

***

Oscar was waiting in the office when Luther and Leanne showed up at eight the next morning.

"Where's Tori?" Luther asked. "I thought she left early to help you in the greenhouses."

"I haven't been there yet," Oscar said. "I wanted to talk to you two first. I know that Tori doesn't want to go back to school. It sort of isn't my business but it sort of is, too. I mean, your family is your business but she's my unofficial assistant. I want to give her a portion of my shares."

"Oh, no, no," Luther said, then halted when Oscar raised his hand. "That's not what I wanted to talk about. I have a family dilemma. I have to fly back to Paris to see my mother." He shrugged his shoulder, not wanting to explain further.

"Understood," Luther said. "Family first. I hadn't made the official phone call to the school about her attendance, but this makes it easier for me, too. I'll just say she has to stay home and help with the family business. Plain and simple. No further explanation required for anyone. I will tell you, though…" Luther got comfortable in his office chair and grabbed a pencil, twirling it between his fingers to help him concentrate. "The parents of that boy who dyed her braid called the school. They wanted to press assault charges."

"What?" Oscar asked.

"Yeah, I wish I'd been there when that happened," Leanne said. "Luther told them that their big football player son attacked her first. All she did was defend herself. With a lock of her own hair!"

"Well, it was a little more than a lock," Luther said, "but not much more. I guess the principal is on our side. There's always been a zero-tolerance for bullying but no way to enforce it. The teachers are too afraid of the students."

"So, how's that going to change?" Oscar asked.

"They were afraid of losing their funding. It turns out that the teacher in that class had submitted a grant request. The school no longer has to depend on endowments from rich parents for sports."

"That doesn't make sense," Oscar said.

"It had something to do with matching funds for academics and sports. Her grant is not tied to any athletic program. But their problems with finances aren't ours. Tori was only attending school so she'd get some people skills and maybe a little exposure to what life was like outside of just the two of us."

"Three of us," Leanne amended.

"Or more," Oscar said. "She's not ducking into dark corners when the trim crew comes in."

Luther chuckled. "Kind of hard to do that in a greenhouse," he said.

"So, since she's got some people skills going and knows what's needed to bring the crops to harvest, I wanted to ask you if she could take over. That's why I wanted to share my cut. We can work the numbers out later or do it right now." Oscar looked around the office. "As soon as we figure out where she went."

"Probably looking for you," Luther said.

"Luther!" Leanne hissed, smacking his arm.

"Oh, and do you think you can give me a ride to the Portland Airport tomorrow? We'd have to leave at," Oscar looked at his watch, "at about ten-thirty."

"AM or PM?"

"AM. I know it's short notice but…"

"Family first," Luther said. "Come on. Let's walk around and see if there are any loose ends that need to be tied up. I think you have more confidence in her than I do."

"Don't tell me: you still think of her as your baby, right?"

"Kind of hard not to."

***

An hour passed and Tori still wasn't around.

Or at least, she was trying to be invisible. After they had done a cursory check on the four dedicated cannabis greenhouses, the men returned to the office. Luther reached into the pile of jackets and coveralls hanging on the wall and pulled Tori out by the upper arm.

"This stops now, young lady," he said. "You're embarrassing me and yourself. And probably Oscar, too. We need you to step up to the plate."

"What does that mean anyhow?" she asked, indignant at being caught.

"It's your turn at bat," Oscar said. "I have to leave tomorrow morning. I need you to take over while I'm gone."

"But…but…why?"

"I have to go take care of my mother. It's not something I necessarily *want* to do but what I *need* to do."

Tori looked at Oscar, then her father, and back at Oscar. "Is she going to die or something?"

"That could happen. Do you want to help me help her? I know you've never met her, but she is a mother. We tend to think of moms as tough and able to take care of the world. But many times, they're not. Often they're as vulnerable as babies."

"Just a lot older," Tori said, frowning.

Luther took his hand off her arm and lifted her face to his. "If your mother needed help, what would you do? Would you drop everything and be there for her or just hope someone else would come by and take care of her?"

Tori paused, thinking about what he had asked. "You're the only one who could take care of Mama as well as I could," she said, then glanced up at him. "And I'm not too sure about that. Yes. I understand. I'll behave and step up to the plate. But I don't have to like it!"

Oscar looked at her. Her bottom lip was stuck out defiantly, her head still covered with the knit cap he had given her the day before. "Look for the good part in any job you do. I know you already like all aspects of growing and harvesting. You'll be doing all the same work we do every day but without me."

Tori sucked back her scowl and lifted her chin. Determined. "I can handle it. Just don't get too used to being gone."

"Now *that* I'll promise."

Chapter 9: The Ultimate Embarrassment

Oscar spent the day making phone calls and scribbling notes in a journal so Tori had a guidebook with names and numbers in case she needed them. But he knew she wouldn't. If she could overcome her aversion to talking on the phone, she'd have the job mastered.

"Go ahead and schedule a harvest crew for greenhouse one for October seventh," Oscar said. "I'll be right here in case you freeze up."

Tori took his kid-glove approach at helping her as a challenge to succeed on her own. She picked up the phone and dialed from memory, then felt her chest tighten. Yup, freeze up.

Oscar reached for the phone but she turned around, denying him access. She coughed once, forcing air into her lungs, then spoke, her voice thin and just above a whisper.

"Sorry 'bout that," she said. She cleared her throat again, her voice now stronger and confident. "I had something stuck. Let me start again. This is Tori Greene at Chill Out Growers. Yes, we're the new grow site right behind If You Can Imagine Vineyards. My partner and I..." She paused, looking over at Oscar to give him a wink, "My partner and I are looking to schedule a crew to come out and harvest three hundred plants. Yes, I know this is the busy time of year and that's why I'm calling early. Really? You booked up that long ago? I was hoping that four-weeks' notice would be enough. Do you have a smaller crew that could come out or can you recommend someone else? Oh, we're not afraid of startups as long as they have good recommendations. All right, put the Dragonfly crew down for the week of the thirtieth. Nah, if you say they're good, I'll believe you. No need to put us on a cancellation list. That's Tori. T-O-R-I. Like Victoria but without the start and finish. Just the good stuff in the middle. Right. Thanks!"

Tori handed the phone back to Oscar and sat down hard in the chair. She leaned forward and covered her face, emotionally spent. "Did I sound like a rambling idiot to you or was that just to me?"

"Tori, you had more confidence than a five-hundred-pound Sumo wrestler coming up against a five-pound Pekinese! I'm so proud of you that I might give you all the phone work."

"Oh, no you don't," she said. "That scared the pee out of me." She sat up quickly and looked at the chair. "Nah. No pee," she said and laughed.

"You're so cute when you're strong," Oscar said, giving her a kiss on the forehead.

"You missed."

He sighed deeply. "When's your birthday again?" he asked although he already knew it was three months away.

"Don't worry. I'm sure if you asked them nicely, my folks would let you take me out on a date. Not that I can think of anywhere I want to go. I mean, I'd rather watch sunsets and DVDs with you – munching on microwave popcorn – than go to a theater."

Tori finished her declaration, then stuck her face up and shut her eyes, waiting for another kiss.

"I'm not sure if I can make sunset tonight," Oscar said, one hand on her shoulders, the other pushing stray hairs behind her ear. "I have to go into town and take care of some business in person." He rolled his eyes. "Lawyers and bankers," he said. "I'll try to be back but you know how traffic is."

"There they are!" Luther said, popping into the office.

Oscar's hands dropped to his side as if the boss had just caught him with his fingers in the till.

Luther looked aside, letting the guilt-ridden young man compose himself. "We'd like you to join us for dinner tonight, Oscar. I know it's your last night but you still have to eat, right?"

"I'm sorry. I have to take care of some legal mumbo jumbo in Portland before I leave the country. Looks like I'll have to eat my first drive-through food since I came to work here."

"Better take some antacids with you," Luther warned. "You never seem to have them when you need them. And there's no worse place to have an upset stomach than when you're stuck in I-5 traffic."

"I'll pick some up when I head into town for fuel. There's no problem taking the work truck, is there?"

"It's your uncle's truck, not mine. I'm not going anywhere, so help yourself."

***

Tori sat at her window, headphones on as she watched for headlights coming up the hill. It was already nine o'clock and he still hadn't returned. Sunsets weren't the same without him. "You're smitten, woman," she said aloud. "Just like a romance novel, hung up on the hero. Hopelessly infatuated with him, yearning for his hands on you…"

She picked up the book she'd been reading. "I gotta stop reading this stuff. Just because every bit of it's true doesn't make it easier to handle. Dang! If you'd asked me a year ago, I'd say these romance stories were as real as Cinderella versus the Vampire! Pure sensationalism!" She took out the bookmark, ready to read again, then looked out the window. Someone had just turned onto their road. It had to be him. No one came out this far who didn't belong.

Tori stood up, grabbed for her flannel shirt, and was stopped short by her corded headphones. "Dang it!" She took them off and threw them on the bed, slipped on her shoes, and opened the door and listened.

"Sing me another song, Luther," her mother cooed.

Ew! I don't know which is worse: the lovemaking or the parts that come before and after it. At least, they're busy and won't know I'm gone.

Tori hopped on her bike and sped to Oscar's trailer, ready to spend some 'quality time' with him. How far would he let her go tonight? Tingles ran up her body as she recalled their passionate make-out session on the picnic blanket, 'not' watching the sun go down. What would have happened if they hadn't been interrupted by that call from his cousin? She reached up and fastened the top button on her flannel against the chill, knowing that the shiver was from thinking about him, not the evening air.

What was the worst that could happen? She knew. She could get pregnant. Would that be so bad? It would mean he'd be in her life forever. Did she want that? Absolutely! Scenarios of possibilities and different love scenes from Mama's romance novels played over in her head, sending shivers up her chest and spine, warming her lady parts as she pedaled furiously to get to his place before he did.

Fwap!

Just as Tori pulled up to Oscar's trailer, the bike chain flew off, sending her skidding into his gravel front yard. As she was kicking the wrecked bike away, the headlights of the truck shone on her.

The engine shut off but the lights stayed on as Oscar jumped out to help her. "Are you all right?"

She looked up at his face. Not a sign of a laugh or a giggle at her pratfall, only concern for her. "I don't know yet. It just happened."

"Here, let me help you get up."

Oscar put his arm under hers and led her up the steps and onto his bed. "Let me shut off the truck lights. Don't try to do anything. I'll be right back and take care of you."

Tears burst out, caused by embarrassment, not pain. That would come later when the stun of the crash wore off and the tenderness of knees and elbows skinned raw took over.

"Oh, man," Oscar said, bringing the flashlight close to her knee. "That looks painful. What happened?"

"Chain broke," she said, sniffing back tears.

"Do you want me to clean it up for you or should I take you home and let your mom deal with it?

"She's busy."

"Okay. How about your dad?"

"They're busy together," she said and rolled her eyes, unable to keep the giggle out of her voice.

"Oh, I see. Or I don't see. I mean…"

"Yeah, best not to think about it. Could you do it for me? I'm not too good at the sight of blood. I'd hate to add barf and make it the ultimate embarrassment."

"No problem. Let me get a basin and squirt bottle."

Oscar gently and compassionately tended to her injuries, enjoying the feel of her skin beneath his hands, her willingness to let him do what he would to her. "Why did you come out so late?" he asked when he was done with the first aid.

"I wanted to spend more time with you." She shrugged her shoulder, looking through his window toward her house and noticed that from his bed, he could look into her bedroom window if her blinds were open. A sly grin grew. He was smitten with her, too. She wouldn't tell him what she'd discovered, though.

"Helluva last night together," he said, adding a nervous chuckle.

"What do you mean? We're together on your bed, aren't we?"

"Tori Lynn Greene!" he exclaimed, then laughed.

"I didn't know you knew my middle name."

"I've heard both your parents call you out with all three names. I guess it isn't Victoria, is it?"

"I used to make jokes that there were really three of me. All together, I was one named Vickie-Tori-Ria. I had heard the name Victoria somewhere and thought that's what it was. Mama said no, my name was just Tori, not Victoria. 'We didn't need the extra at the beginning and the end,' she said."

"Well, Vickie-Tori-Ria, do you want me to drive you back tonight or do you think you can drive yourself? I still have to pack."

"I'm just Tori," she said, remembering the photo of Mama nursing her. *So much for being one of three…*

"So…" Oscar prompted her when they were standing next to the truck. "Drive yourself or I'll drive?"

"I got this," she said, her hand out for the keys.

"Yeah, well you may have been in my bed tonight, but know this, you'll be in my heart every night while I'm gone. I'll set up that app that Rich used so we can talk. There's a nine-hour time difference so you'll have to call me before noon."

"I don't have a smartphone," she said, trying not to start crying again.

"No worries. That's one thing I stopped off for when I was in town. I'll get it set up for you in the morning. For right now, though, I really need to pack and then get some sleep. I'm wiped out."

Tori twirled the keyring around her finger. "Yeah, me, too. Wiped out after wiping out. Either Papa or I will pick you up tomorrow at seven. Is that too early?"

"It's never too early to see you," he said, then kissed her on the top of the head.

"Yeah," she said, then carefully stepped into the truck. *I'll give you an hour or so to pack, and then I'll be back!*

Tori pulled up to the house, turned off the headlights, then sat, wondering if she should go in. Mama and Papa's bedroom was dark. They were asleep. Not even the gentle glow of the candles Mama lit for their time together was visible. She pulled her shirt together, glad that she had worn one of her heavier ones. It was still summer by the calendar, but early September evenings were cool, especially after ten o'clock at night. She looked over at Oscar's trailer. His lights were off now, too.

Hoping her parents wouldn't hear the sound of the truck starting, she drove up the hill slowly, looking back at her house to make sure the lights stayed off. Great. Her parents were still asleep.

The only sound she heard as she stopped a hundred feet from Oscar's place was the chirping of frogs. *Great! Cover noise for the crunch of gravel.*

She walked to the house. Still in the front yard was the mangled mess of the bike she'd ridden since she was eight years old. Definitely time for some new wheels. The sparkle of the pink unicorn sticker reflected in the brightness of the full moon. She'd get some goop and transfer it to her new ride, though. She paused at the top of the three steps into the trailer, the frogs stilled by her presence. She listened for sounds from Oscar. Nothing. Cool. He didn't snore like Papa.

Glad that he never locked his door, Tori slipped inside, soundlessly closing it behind her.

Neat and tidy as always, Oscar had cleaned up the mess from doctoring her, tossing the bandage packaging into the garbage. The basin had been washed and dried, ready for cut-up watermelon, chips, or salads. His home would be clean and ready when he returned.

Tori carefully set the keys on the hook on the wall, slipped off her shoes, and tiptoed over to his bed. He slept on the side of the double bed closest to the window, a gentle breeze blowing across his bare-chested body. She inhaled deeply, memorizing the scent that was already familiar to her. Unclothed, it was stronger, more enticing. She noticed one of his shirts tossed on top of a laundry basket, the denim one he'd been wearing when he performed first aid. There was a smear of her blood on it. It was too soiled to wear without pretreating and washing, but in much better shape than the ripped and dirty flannel she was wearing. She put on his shirt and tossed hers in the basket. She'd take it with her when she left. Right now, her shoulders were cold.

As quietly as if she was sneaking an acorn from a sleeping squirrel, Tori pulled back the lightweight thermal blanket and crawled beneath it. Oscar made a small noise of discomfort, then readjusted his shoulders into the pillow and fell back into his deep sleep.

All she wanted to do was see him one more time. Be close to him. They didn't even have to talk. She took in all she could of his appearance with just the moonlight from the window. His hair was short but just a little wild. She still had his hat. He hadn't asked for it back. Hopefully, he never would. If he asked, she'd tell him she wanted to wash it first. She definitely didn't want to do that but that's what she'd say. It smelled of him. She inhaled again, his bare shoulders so close to her. Why was a man's scent so attractive? Why would women spend hundreds of dollars on perfumes when a person's natural aroma was nature's way of pointing mates in the right direction.

Mates. She shuddered. They had all the time in the world to get to know each other. He didn't know when he'd be back but they were partners. Mates of the clothing-required type…

She hadn't meant to fall asleep and didn't realize she had until a fly landed on her lip. She sputtered, hoping she didn't swallow it.

"What the hell?" Oscar jumped out of bed and grabbed his pillow to cover his nakedness. "What are you doing here?"

"You were naked?" she asked.

"Yeah, I always sleep without clothes on. You didn't answer my question. What are you doing here?"

Tori stood up and turned away from him, the pain of her bruises and abrasions zipping through her body, embarrassed all over again that she had done something stupid. "I…I…" she looked down and realized she was wearing his shirt. "I came to get your shirt. I'll get the bloodstain out of it for you."

"You have to go home. Now. Tori, you don't understand what a big deal this is. I could get arrested and sent to prison for this. I know we didn't do anything…" He paused, trying to remember what happened before he went to bed. "I'm sure we didn't do anything, but just being in the same room could land me in jail, especially with me naked, for God's sake!"

"I'm sorry, I'm sorry," Tori kept repeating, stumbling over the laundry basket as she tried to pull her shirt out of it.

"Just go. And don't tell anyone you were here. I'm serious. Your dad could not only have me arrested, he might also shoot me!"

Tori stumbled down the steps in tears, disoriented. She spotted her crashed bike, confused about how she had arrived, then spotted the truck.

And her father.

Luther was pulling up in the Gator, his broad-brimmed hat shadowing his angry face. "What's going on here, young lady. Or should I say, young woman?"

"It's all my fault. Don't shoot him. Don't have him arrested. He didn't do anything. We didn't do anything. I promise. I'm so stupid!" Tori blurted out between heavy sobs and tears.

Luther looked up and saw Oscar at the open door in sweatpants and no shirt. "What's going on here?"

"I told you, Papa, nothing!" Tori screamed. "It's all me! I'm so stupid…"

"Go home, Tori. Your mother's worried sick about you. I'm going to have a talk with Oscar."

"But Papa…"

"Go! Now!" he growled.

Oscar stepped back out of the doorway, letting Luther come in. He didn't make a sound. Nothing he could say would help the situation.

Luther sat down at the small kitchenette table, snorting in rage, taking deep breaths to contain his rage. He looked up at Oscar and saw a total lack of emotion and felt compassion.

"She came in and you didn't even know it, right?"

Oscar nodded but remained mute.

"You didn't do anything to her, right?"

He nodded again, then reached over to flip on the coffee pot.

"What am I going to do with that girl?"

Oscar opened his mouth to speak, then paused. He looked at the distraught parent. "Keep loving her and don't alienate her."

He saw Luther's shoulders relax and added, "And maybe put a lock on her bedroom door and window."

"Lord Almighty, I'm glad it was you and not some young buck out for thrills," Luther huffed.

"She came over to see me after I got back from Portland. She said the chain came off her bike. I'm pretty sure that's what happened because she skidded across the yard and really did a number on her knees and elbows. I doctored her up and sent her home in the truck. I guess I should have escorted her."

"Hindsight's twenty-twenty," Luther said. "How about if I hang out here while that coffee's brewing. It's still early yet. I'll let her stew a bit, let her mama chew on her and soften her up so she doesn't repeat the same mistake for a while."

"Well, you won't have to worry about me for a few months. It looks like my mother's losing her mind. Again. They want to commit her to an institution. I want to spend some time with her and see if I can pull her head out of her southern realm. She didn't take it well when my dad left."

"Take as much time as you want. We'll still be here when you get back. At least, I hope you come back. Tori may have made a big mistake, but there's no use in cutting out her heart. She's mighty fond of you, you know."

"That goes both ways. I have to tell you, though, when I woke up, buck naked and with her by my side…"

"What? You were naked in bed with my daughter?" Luther screeched, riled up anew.

"That's how I went to sleep!" Oscar hollered back with nearly as much vigor. "I always do! I didn't expect anyone to join me!"

Luther settled down slightly, then started laughing. "I can't imagine how you felt, going to sleep a single man, then waking up with a seventeen-year-old in bed next to you. Damn! I'll bet you were confused."

"Yeah, you may think it's funny, but put yourself in my place!"

Luther's face fell. "Yeah, I guess that's right. I suppose that would either mean a prison sentence or a shotgun wedding."

"The first terrifies me, the second…" Oscar thought about it for a brief moment. "Well, at least it was Tori and not some woman I didn't know or care for."

"You got that right. Go ahead and get showered and dressed or whatever you need to do. I'll wait for the coffee to finish and give Leanne time to chastise that wayward daughter of ours. Still going to the airport at ten-thirty?"

"As long as she hasn't crashed the truck, too. I don't think that Gator would make the minimum speed limit on the freeway."

Chapter 10: Emotional Hangover

Honk! Honk!

Luther waited a minute for Oscar then got out of the truck when he didn't come out of his trailer. He looked at his watch again. They were running late. The ten minutes he'd spent trying to convince Tori to join them hadn't helped.

When Luther walked in, Oscar looked up, startled. "Sorry. I guess I was off in my own little world. I didn't hear you pull up. I couldn't find my paperwork. Here it is!" He pulled out a bulging shipping envelope from the shelf above his bed. "I knew I put it in a safe place, but you know how that goes. By the time I put it away last night, I was exhausted. I'm glad I found it." He glanced around, unplugged the coffee pot, then patted himself down, checking his pockets. "Passport, ticket, power of attorney... Yeah, I'm set."

Luther climbed in the truck and watched in sympathy as the anxious young man stood at the top of the steps, searching for Tori. "She's not here," he sighed in frustration.

"What? She didn't want to come with us?" Oscar asked.

"Would you want to be stuck in the front of a truck with someone who'd just witnessed your most humiliating and embarrassing moment ever?"

"I guess not. I didn't even get to show her the phone I bought her. Would you give it to her? I left it on the kitchen counter with a bow and a note on it, telling her we can video chat with it."

"You could have saved yourself a lot of money. We can do that with our old desktop computer, too."

"I know but it's a lot more personal when you don't have to be at work to talk..." Oscar chopped off the end of his sentence before he got to 'with your boyfriend.'

Luther noticed the awkward halt but didn't comment on it. "She's still wounded. It's her own damned fault, though!"

"Think of it as she's hit a growth spurt. It's an emotional one, but

103

she's still adjusting to new feelings. She never had any power over anything or anyone. Suddenly, she's in charge. Or at least she thinks she is."

"What are you talking about?"

"Okay, try to back away from the fact that she's your daughter, and embrace the part where I'm your co-worker explaining my dilemma. Just for grins, let's call her Suzy."

"That was the name she gave all her goldfishes, but okay. Go ahead."

"So, I have a girlfriend, mostly platonic. She wants to do more, but I know she's both too young and vulnerable."

"And inexperienced," Luther added with a throaty huff.

Oscar ignored the man's protective growl. "So, Suzy and I kissed one day. That's all. Both fully clothed, nothing below the belt or anything like that."

Another guttural growl but Oscar saw that the possessive papa was still holding it together.

"Suzy wants more. Oscar does, too, but absolutely, positively won't give in."

"Good man. He'll live longer that way."

"Exactly. But what's he supposed to do about Suzy? While he was asleep, she sneaked in and crawled into his bed. She could have put him in prison for life if her father had been the unreasonable sort."

Luther sighed, stroking the steering wheel as if it was a cat he was trying to calm down, but it was his own nerves he was working on. "Evidently the man knew his daughter very well. Yes, sounds like Suzy needs to take a time out. Hmm. How long did you say you were going to be gone?"

"I didn't because I don't know."

"I understand what you're saying about Suzy, so listen to my story about Tori. She's different. She lives in her own magical world. I'd love to see her have a normal life. You know that I care for you, right? Don't get me wrong, I'm not trying to thrust her on you, but I don't want to see her hurt either. I don't think she'd ever recover. She's already reeling from just this morning."

Luther signaled a lane change and switched topics, too. "I don't think you're aware that it wasn't until you arrived in our lives that she stopped spending so much time in her imaginary world."

"You mean the one where she talks to *the others*?" Oscar asked hesitantly.

"You know about that, I mean, *them*?"

"Yeah, when we were little, I overheard her talking to her reflection in a stock tank. She seemed to think there really was someone there. I don't think she ever knew I heard her conversation. At least, I never said anything about it to anyone until now. Even then I knew how vulnerable she was. Like a little fairy princess who – if I said the wrong words – would flit away and never come back. I didn't want that. I mean, I wasn't going to be responsible for crushing someone's spirit or essence, that's for sure."

"Thanks. I appreciate that. Yes, she has two imaginary friends. She never talks about them to us. She tried when she was small but hasn't brought them up since she went to kindergarten. I guess she told her little friend and the teacher about them. The teacher told us about it at our conference. She said not to worry, that she'd outgrow it. I don't know whether she has or hasn't. Like I said, it's something we don't talk about."

"I see she put my hat in the truck. Here, give it back to her, please. Tell her I said I want her to keep it so her ears will stay warm until her hair grows out. I'll be back. I promise. I don't know when but make sure she knows that I will."

Luther sighed but didn't say a word.

"I understand her like not many others possibly could, Luther. Other than my mother, Tori is the most important woman in my world. I have to take care of Mom, though. You see, she's another fairy princess. I don't want to hurt her, either."

***

"She still won't take the phone?" Oscar asked, video calling from France.

"Won't even look at it," Luther said into the desktop monitor, shaking his head in frustration.

"Same thing on the cards and letters?"

"They're in a pile at the corner of her desk, untouched. She still comes to work but now that the harvest and trimming are done, she just mopes around, sweeping floors, watching the goldfish swim in the tank, dusting empty shelves. I really don't have anything for her to do. I'd love to take her and the missus on a vacation. Since the vineyards are done for the winter and we're not planting more cannabis until spring, I could hire a caretaker to watch the place. Tori's here but she's empty, like a pillowcase without the pillow."

"Blowing in the wind without any substance or purpose," Oscar said. "Dang. On the upside, my mother is responding to the new shrink. He's weaned her off almost all of her meds, making sure she exercises daily, gets fresh air and sunshine, and keeps away from all alcohol and sugar. The sugar is the hardest part for her, being in France and all. She never cared for wine, so that's not a real problem. Whiskey and tequila aren't easy for her to find, especially since I made sure she didn't get a drivers' license."

"Well, keep checking in. If something changes, I'll call."

"Do me a favor, Luther. Go ahead and set up her new phone with this app we're talking on. Set it in her room where it's not too obvious. If she's having a good day, let me know. I'll pop in. I know from dealing with my mother that timing is everything. You have to smile when they're looking."

"I hear you there. Thanks for checking in, Oscar. Roger, over and out."

Leanne stepped into the office. "Did I just hear Oscar?"

Luther chuckled and pointed to the computer. "Right there. He said to set up that new phone he got Tori. Don't tell her. We're hoping to catch her on a good day. He's either a saint or an idiot the way he

106

chases after her."

"Hmph!" Leanne snorted. "Wouldn't you have chased me this long if it was us and not them."

"Yeah, I suppose I would."

"You suppose!" she said indignantly, then laughed. "Don't worry about it. I'm the one you chased until I caught you, remember?"

"Very much so," he said, holding her in a full-body embrace. "How about we take a vacation?"

Leanne grinned. "Sounds like perfect timing. Remember Chuck?"

"Chuck who?" Luther asked with a scowl of suspicion.

"I never knew his last name. Let's just say remember the angel who delivered our child?"

"Oh, yeah! Gloria and Roger's friend. Hell ya, I remember him! If he hadn't jumped in the middle of our," Luther whispered the word, "adoption," then shook his head, leaving off the rest of the story she already knew.

"Yes. You're right. He's the sole reason we're a family of three today," Leanne said. "He never asked us for anything. Not that we had anything to give him, but he's asking a favor now. It seems that Gloria's daughter is getting married at the end of the month. Somehow or another, the birth mother and Tori's two sisters are all in each other's lives. Everyone is cool, no contested you-know-whats," she said, then whispered, "custody disputes."

She took a deep breath and smiled, recalling their early years. "Chuck just wants to give Vickie the gift of meeting the other sister she's known about for two years. Actually, Ria – that's Chuck's daughter – is the maid of honor and will be there, too. He never said anything about us to anyone earlier because he had promised discretion. He's certainly given it!"

"Do you think Tori will agree to go on a vacation? And are you sure she's strong enough to know about the others?" Luther asked.

"Pbbt! On the first one. I'm not giving her a choice. She's

coming! Plus, that girl's so mad at us now, what's the worst that could happen when she finds out she was adopted? I don't want to say anything beforehand, just let the girls meet each other. Tori will figure it out."

"But I thought we weren't ever going to tell her," Luther said, frowning in disappointment. He paused, remembering that she was a woman now and could probably handle the truth. "Ah, what the hell. Maybe it will shock her into reality. This depression or anger – or whatever the hell it is – has been going on for almost three months. It's time for it to end."

"Oh, and this just came in the mail," Leanne said, handing him an official-looking plastic envelope.

Luther used his knife to open the overpack that read 'Damaged in processing equipment.' He opened the second and third envelopes. "Well, lookie there." He held up the torn inner card. "It's a wedding invitation from Rick Rickman. His son, Rich, is getting married. Hey, Gloria's daughter's name is Vickie, right?"

"Yes, Vickie Lynn Thornwhistle."

"Looks like the young lady is marrying well. She's the one marrying Rick's kid. You do remember Oscar's cousin Rich, right? I guess we got our unofficial invitation to the wedding before the real deal. We can sit on either the bride or the groom's side!"

"Ah, I'd say going to the wedding was meant to be," Leanne said. "That makes me feel better about the revelation already." She scowled at Luther. "But I still don't want to be the one to tell her!"

"You and me, both," Luther said. "Maybe we made a mistake and maybe we didn't by leading her on. Either way, she's going to be mad that we didn't tell her sooner. Mum's still the word for now, though. I don't want her to blow up while we're driving cross country. I don't think that truck could contain her rage!"

***

January 30, 2010

"I think this is the place," Luther said, verifying the address on

108

the invitation.

"It's about time," Tori grumbled. "You didn't tell me it was going to take four days to get here!"

"It was only three and a half. How long did you think it would take to cross the whole United States in a truck? In winter!"

"Hmph!"

Leanne looked at the clock in the dash for the hundredth time in the last two hours. "We made it in plenty of time, but it looks like everyone else is already here."

Luther had an aha moment. "Did you remember to take into consideration the last time zone change?"

"Oh, shoot!"

Luther didn't say a word. What good would it have done? Instead, he drove around to the back of the reception hall, looking for an open parking place. He saw a man waving at him. "Is that Chuck?" he asked.

"Oh, my! It is. Look, he saved us a spot."

Leanne unbuckled and was ready to get out before Luther even had the engine turned off. "Oh, it is you!" she squealed, rushing into Chuck's open arms. "Are we too late?"

"It's just getting ready to start." He looked up and saw Luther standing beside the truck, talking to the other occupant, apparently discussing whether or not she would be leaving the vehicle. "Is everything okay?" he asked Leanne.

"He can handle her. At least, he can do it better than I can. She's stubborn. Just give him a minute…"

The two stood close, sharing each other's warmth, and watched silently as the insistent father tried reasoning with his reluctant daughter. A moment later, Luther was escorting her by the elbow. Chuck tried not to stare at the angry young woman as she approached, so alike in physical features to his own daughter and her sister. He'd seen that glare of defiance many times over the past eighteen years, but she had something else showing through. He couldn't put a finger on it, but she was different.

The four walked into the back of the wedding hall. "Go ahead and sit here in the last row. If anyone asks, you were invited by the family of the bride. The Thornwhistles don't know you're coming, though. I asked them to make sure they left room for a few spares. Just act like you belong, because you do!" he said, patting the insecure Leanne on her shoulder.

He turned around and saw that Tori had disappeared again. "She won't go far, will she?" he asked Leanne.

"No, she's bashful but not a runner." She looked over at the cluttered coat rack and saw movement. "Two to one she's in there. Don't worry. She didn't want to come but can't go anywhere without us. She may be eighteen, but she doesn't know how to drive on anything but farm roads."

"Shush!" Luther hissed. "Dang! It's over. That's about the quickest wedding I've ever been to."

"It's the only wedding – other than our own – you've ever been to," Leanne said. "Now come on and let's get our daughter. I want to meet the bride and groom…and that beautiful young bridesmaid!"

Luther, Leanne, and Chuck stepped back and applauded, marveling at the beautiful women and their handsome escorts as they walked down the center aisle in reverse, following the strewn rose petals into the reception hall. "Oh, and we did have an invitation," Luther said, pulling out the rumpled card and showing it to Chuck. "I work for the groom's father. We're here for Rich, too!"

***

Tori remained hidden behind plain and fur-trimmed coats, her back pressed close to the wall as she tried to make herself invisible. She moved a jacket sleeve out of the way, still curious enough about what was going on to peek out and investigate. This wasn't a church but was just as busy with people all dressed up and milling around, babbling – talking to each other without saying anything significant. She let the sleeve fall back in place and stepped back, shoulder blades to the wall.

She heard her mother's voice call to her softly. "Come out and meet my friends."

Rats! She found me.

"I can see you plain as day," Leanne said, then whispered, "Come on, sweetheart. You're embarrassing your papa and me." She looked to her husband. "Grab your daughter, Luther. She won't come otherwise."

Tori squirmed in the confines of the musty woolen and polyester outerwear hanging on the bar above her. She didn't want to leave, but she didn't want to make a scene, either. *It's going to be okay. It's going to be okay. Just smile and nod. They promised it would be just a few minutes, and then we could go home.*

Suddenly, she felt her father's grasp on her upper arm. "Come on, sweetheart. No one here's going to bite you."

"Can't we go home now, Papa?" she mumbled.

"Give us a few minutes. We drove for three and a half days to get here. Let your mama and me have at least a little time to chat with our old friends. Come meet a few of them. Not all of them. Just a few special ones."

"But I really, really want to go home now," Tori whispered.

"There's nothing but rain and gloom out there now. If you come out willing and behave, I promise you a surprise like nothing you've ever seen or expected."

"Well, she may have seen," Leanne said, "but she certainly isn't expecting this. At least, in this format."

"What are you two babbling about?" Tori asked, her curiosity piqued. "You know I can't resist a mystery."

"Ah, you're right there. Come on. And take off that silly hat!"

Tori pulled off Oscar's knit cap, her blonde hair flying everywhere with static electricity. "Now, show me something I didn't expect," she said. "Because you know I have a pretty vivid imagination."

Suppressing her urge to bolt, Tori sucked it up and followed, curious again about the mystery of seeing something familiar in a new way. A grin grew at the adventure. It couldn't be them, could it?

Tori looked around the room, her smile of anticipation as warm and bright as the mood of the people. It was a wedding. She loved weddings. At least, reading about them. This was the first one she'd ever been to. Or almost been to. She grunted with disgust at herself. Her shyness had stolen her joy again. When would she ever outgrow it? 'One of these days' her parents always said. Well, she'd just have to choose a day. And today – with all these positive vibes, happy voices, and joyous music, the smell of fragrant food and warmth of bodies moving around stress and anger-free – this was a good day to claim moodiness was dead. Long live joy and hope!

Tori looked up. They had stopped. "This is my former college roommate, Gloria," Leanne said, pulling her daughter forward. "And this is Tori Lynn Greene."

Suddenly close to a stranger, Tori panicked and popped back into the security of her shyness shell, wishing she could run home all by herself. She hung her head and pressed her chin tight to her chest so she didn't have to look into the beautiful woman's eyes. Maybe today wasn't the right day to try and stomp out moodiness after all.

The stunned mother of the bride blinked several times at seeing the terrified young woman. Moments ago when Leanne had come up to say hi, she half-expected to see Tori with her. The two women hadn't seen each other in over eighteen years – since the night they picked out their babies from Chuck's smuggled gym bag. But the triplet sister was here now. She was so similar to the others but at the same time, so different. *Definitely assembled from the same genetic code. But unlike Vickie and Ria, this one apparently didn't even get a smidgen of the generous dose of confidence the other two had.*

Gloria quickly recognized the girl's shyness as anxiety and decided she might be the only one who could help her. Ignoring her own daughter and the rest of the wedding party for the moment, she reached over and put her hand on the frightened young girl's shoulder. "Let's go into the cloakroom, shall we? There are so many people in here, it has to be overwhelming for a small-town girl."

Leanne and Tori silently followed Gloria into the calmness of the small annex, the loft of the coats and jackets acting as soundproofing from the tumultuous din of the wedding guests in the main hall. Already feeling more comfortable back in her old hideout, Tori reached up and touched a mink coat, marveling at its softness. "Why did they kill them? Don't people know that these creatures need their fur, too? Wool can be just as warm or warmer and it's a renewable resource. You don't have to kill the sheep to get it."

"Tori Lynn!" Leanne scolded. "It is not your place to tell people what they should or shouldn't wear. Now, you've barely been introduced and you're criticizing? I swear, sometimes it's better when you don't talk."

"She might be right, you know," Gloria said to Leanne. "These aren't mine, so I don't know if they're real or synthetic. Either way, I prefer wool in the winter, cotton in the summer. How about you, Tori?"

"Same here," Tori said, her shyness evaporating like mist on a campfire at having the stranger agree with her. "See," she opened up her gray woolen jacket to reveal a blue plaid flannel shirt and white cotton tank top. "I like cotton, too."

"My goodness," Gloria said, excited at the girl's rapid recovery. "If you had arrived half an hour earlier, you could have been in the wedding! The bridesmaids were wearing flannel, too!"

"In a wedding… I don't know," Leanne said. "She's not too keen on strangers."

"Strangers? Well, Tori, my name is Gloria Thornwhistle and I don't want to be a stranger. I have a daughter the same age as you. When things settle down, I'd like you to meet her. As far as meeting new people, you're just going to have to trust your parents to have good friends."

"Trust those trusted by those I trust?" Tori asked, then answered her own question. "Yes, ma'am. I can try that, at least for today. Mama and Papa said I was going to meet some very special people here. They promised me it would be a short trip, though." She looked down at her watch, the black faux leather band similar to everything else about her: simple and uncomplicated. "There's three hours difference between here and Oregon, you know," she said, a mischievous grin on her face.

"Tori Lynn Greene!" Leanne hissed. "It's rude to watch the clock when you're in a social setting."

"But that's the truth. Plus, you're the one who said they're friends. Gloria understands me, I'm sure."

"You are a little minx, aren't you?" Gloria said, impulsively hugging her as if she was Vickie or Ria.

"Yes, I suppose I am. But do you think that's a good characteristic?"

Gloria nodded emphatically, holding back the tears of joy. "I definitely want you to meet my daughter and her sister. You'll see that you three have a lot in common."

Leanne looked up at Gloria and paled. "But...but...I think I changed my mind. It might be better if they don't meet."

"Too late. I got this," Gloria said. "Let's go find them."

Clink! Clink! Clink!

The women stepped out of the cloakroom and looked to see who was trying to get everyone's attention. It was Luther's boss, Rick Rickman. "It's about time he showed up," Tori whispered.

"Hush!" Leanne hissed.

All eyes went to the father of the bride, rapping his knife on the side of a crystal glass. "Here's to Mr. and Mrs. Richard Rickman," he announced when the chatter had stopped. "Health and happiness – and a bit of prosperity – to our very own Rich and Vickie Rickman!"

Tori sneaked a glimpse at the bride. She'd been so intent on hiding that she hadn't been curious about who Rich was marrying or what she looked like. She looked oddly familiar, though. Her young blonde bridesmaid – wearing jeans and flannel just like she was – was giving her a big hug now. It looked like the bride was hugging the bride! That's what was odd. They were twins. Identical twins.

Those two aren't identical twins! They're two of triplets. Except for the hair, we all look alike! I'm a triplet and they're my sisters!

Blood drained from her face and her knees felt weak. She leaned into her mother, clutching her arm for support. "Mom? What's going on?"

"Is this a surprise or what?" Leanne asked. She was definitely caught up in the moment, giddy with excitement, happy that she hadn't protested too much about letting Tori know their secret.

"Do I have sisters you didn't tell me about?"

"Well, yes. Sort of…"

Tori realized that her father was now standing next to her.

"Papa, did you know about this?"

"Yes, well, sort of…"

Tori glared at them. Adrenaline surged and she felt the blood rush back to her muscles. She walked away from parents. Radiating a fierce determination that parted the crowd in front of her like Moses marching through the Red Sea, Tori strode up to the pair of women at the podium.

Chin up, Tori stood in front of them and thrust her hand out in greeting. "Hi," she said boldly. "I think I'm your sister, Tori. I mean, I'm Tori, and I think I'm your sister."

"Tori!" Ria and Vickie exclaimed, then reached out to grab her close. "We heard there was a third but didn't know where to find you or even your last name. How did you know where to find us?"

Chuck stepped up to the exuberant trio. "Vickie, this is your wedding gift: meeting your other sister. Well, I guess it's an engagement gift to you, Ria, and just a surprise to you, Tori."

"But why did you wait so long?" the bride asked Chuck.

"I couldn't do or say anything without permission from Luther and Leanne." Chuck held his hand above his eyebrows and scanned the room, finally spotting the elderly couple. He waved them up. "It took a long time to find them. We thought they were still on the east coast. I think Silas found about two thousand places they *weren't* before starting on the west coast."

"Oregon," Tori said simply. "Eventually." She turned to her sisters. "So, I'm not crazy, right?"

"Why would you think that?" Ria asked.

"Because, well, you know how you can look in the mirror and see your other self? Didn't it ever seem weird, like you should be able to just reach in and grab that other person and pull her out to stand beside you instead of in front of you?"

"Well, kinda," Vickie said, "but I thought everyone felt like that."

"Maybe they do, but I felt something was still missing. Then we moved into a place that had a double mirror in the bathroom. I could move it just so, and then there'd be three of me: me and the two images. It felt so right. I used to get in trouble because I'd take so long in the bathroom. I'd be in there, carrying on conversations in a low voice so no one else would hear. Or rather, my parents wouldn't.

"I always wondered if Mama and Papa were my real parents, too, because I didn't look like either one of them. Plus, they were a little old. Mama even showed me a picture Papa had taken of her nursing me. I'm not quite sure how that was possible, but since Papa can make hair grow on a turnip with the right herbal concoction, then I guess he could have put something together so Mom could get milk."

Tori hooked an arm into each sister's, glad all over again that she wasn't crazy, that there really were two on this earthly plane who looked like her. "So, yes or no: are our biological parents here?"

"Yes," Ria and Vickie answered, then looked at each other with raised eyebrows. *Tori looks like us, but she sure is different!*

Tori scanned the room and spotted Grace and Dusty. The couple was staring at the three of them, misty-eyed, hugging each other. She nodded, acknowledging them. "That was a no-brainer," she said softly. "Even if we didn't look like them, the reaction on their faces proves it. So, I guess I'll hear the whole story about why they gave us up later. Let me see if I can pick out a grandma or grandpa…"

"We don't have a grandma here," Vickie said. "She's sorta *persona non grata* and also out of the country."

"Fair enough. Everyone has a skeleton or two in the closet. Best to leave them alone, I say." Tori kept looking, bypassing the one older gentleman who looked as interested as her biological parents but not alike physically. She spotted Silas and noticed his ears, broad shoulders and regal stance. "Him!" she said with complete confidence.

"Nope," Vickie said. "Him," and pointed to Hal. "He's our mother Grace's dad. It's kind of hard not to notice Grace is our mother. She's almost like an older triplet. Or would that be quadruplet?"

Tori shook off the discussion on the mother. "Nope. I'll bet three DNA tests to a donut that he," she said, this time pointing right to Silas, "is Grace's biological father. The other guy definitely has an emotional investment in all of us, but *he's* her father and our grandfather."

Silas watched as the latest triplet to come into his life pointed at him as she carried on an intense conversation with her sisters. Thirty-seven years after Victoria had gotten him drunk and had her way with him, he'd been busted. He looked over the room, pretending to scout out the crowd in general but really looking at Hal's expression. Grace's father was looking right at him, crestfallen. He knew.

Hal walked over to him. "I always wondered if I was her bio-dad," he said. "It was rumored that Victoria was sowing her last wild oats the week before the wedding, but I always hoped it was just a rumor she started so I'd think she was in demand by others. I didn't want to believe there was any chance another man was Grace's father. It's kind of hard to ignore the family resemblance between you two, but I convinced myself that you were either some long, lost cousin or her ears were a result of a recessive gene popping in. Well, if it was to be anyone, I'm glad it was you."

"Did you ever wonder why I never have more than one drink?" Silas asked.

"And did you ever wonder why I did?" Hal asked, answering his question with his own.

"Do you forgive me?" Silas asked.

"For what? Getting tricked by Victoria? Shit! I'm jealous. You got off easy. I had to live with the bitch for nearly nineteen years!"

Silas tried to hold back his laugh, then saw that Hal was giving into his, so joined him. "We weren't the only two. It's not my place to name names, but she was pretty loose there for a week or two. But you're right. It had to be me. I never realized it, though, until Grace came into the Armstrong family. When she showed up with Victoria, crashing Papa Doc's party, I knew she had to be my issue. Actually, when she started dating Alex, I was glad she was mine."

"So, Papa Doc really was one of the others, then?" Hal asked, tight-lipped.

Silas shrugged his shoulder. "Yes, we both had a butt-pucker moment when we saw Grace and Alex hanging all over each other. We didn't want half-siblings getting carried away. We never said anything directly to each other, but when I saw Papa Doc do a double-take, looking at her ears and then mine, I knew he knew. It was kind of funny, both of us exhaling at the same moment as realization hit." Silas noticed Hal was still grim-faced.

"You are and always have been Grace's daddy. I'm just happy to be one of the honorary grandpas to the girls. And now there's one more. By the looks she was giving me, she figured it out within two minutes of being here."

"Well, she is your granddaughter. It looks like she got more than the ears from you. She's pretty damned perceptive."

Silas sighed then grinned. "Never a daddy, but now an acknowledged granddaddy. I'm sure glad no one in this family gives

118

two flips about whose blood flows through who."

"Back at ya," Hal said.

"Excuse me, excuse me," a young man said, pushing past the two men, rushing toward the three sisters as if he was a doctor and one of them was having a heart attack.

"Who's that?" Silas asked. "I thought I knew everyone here."

"That's Rich's cousin, Oscar. He and his mother were able to come at the last moment."

"Oh, yeah. She's the one who's been spending time at that French resort."

"Resort, clinic, rehab," Hal said, shrugging his shoulder. "She's Rick Rickman's sister and he'd do anything for her."

Silas looked back to see what was going on in the other direction. Often the excitement wasn't where the person was headed but where he had come from. The tall African American woman was watching Oscar, a sly smile of pride on her face. *She obviously has an emotional investment in the man. Her son, maybe?*

"Tori?" Oscar asked, pulling her shoulder toward him so he could look into her face. "You came!"

"Why are *you* here?" she asked indignantly. She looked back at her sisters and their beaus. "And did you know about them? That I had sisters?"

"Not until a few minutes ago…"

"I thought you were in France, taking care of your mother," Tori said harshly, not giving him a chance to explain.

"I was! We – Mom and I – just got here! I didn't see the bride and bridesmaid until the wedding started. I knew that Rich's fiancée looked a lot like you because I saw her in the background of a video chat I had with him a few months ago. You're not identical, though. I mean, there is a definite similarity," Oscar said, looking at the two women he now knew were Tori's sisters.

"I don't look like her?" Tori asked, looking at the bride. She snorted in derision.

"Well, you look more like her," Oscar said, nodding to Ria the bridesmaid, moving his ear forward like hers. "Rich's wife, not so much. Let's just say you may look a lot alike on the outside, but your vibes are very different."

"And so's our hair," Tori said, frustrated that she was so plain.

The groom spotted Oscar and Tori. "Hey, Tori! Long time, no see," Rich said. "I didn't know you were a triplet! Good Lord, I only knew you as a kid, blonde and frisky as a cat with a bell on its tail. I had no idea you'd grow up to be such a beauty. I mean, I guess I'd better tell you right now in case you haven't figure it out. I'm married to your sister."

"Only one of them, I hope," Tori said, scowling.

The conversation between them suddenly stopped. All three watched as a very pregnant woman came up to Ria. Words were said, then the two were involved in an extremely emotional reunion, full of hugs and tears. Their excitement was spilling over but not making any sense to Rich, Tori, or Oscar.

Tori punched Rick in the upper arm and said, "I'm joking," breaking the tension between them. "Geez!"

The two men both breathed a sigh of relief. Rich turned to Oscar and gave him a hearty smack on the shoulder, happy to see the cousin he hadn't seen in five years. "Hey, cuz, glad you could make it. Did you say your mom came, too?"

Grateful that Rich had diverted the conversation and rescued him from the rest of Tori's scolding, Oscar nodded in his mother's direction. "Yup. Look at her. Healthy and radiant..."

"I don't know what went on there and don't need to," Rich said. "She's always looked beautiful to me."

"Trust me. It was touch and go there for a while," Oscar said. "Come on, Tori. I think it's time you met my mother."

"I'm still mad at you," Tori said, resisting his proffered hand.

He put his arm around her shoulder and kissed her on the top of her flyaway hair, sputtering as it tickled his nose. "Don't you think

I'm the one who should be mad at you for what you did? Your little stunt could have landed me in jail or got me shot. But I'm not. Life's too short for anger." He bent close to her ear. "Just think of how many kisses we could have shared."

She pulled away a little bit, not willing to break away completely – he still felt wonderful – and said, "But you were in another country, on another continent."

"True, but we're here together now. Can we be friends again?"

Tori bumped into his chest with the side of her head, closing the gap between them with a gentle, physical exclamation point. "Maybe more. I'm eighteen now."

Oscar barely heard her last declaration over the noise of the gathering and was just introducing her to his mother when it registered what she had said. "Ma...Mom," he sputtered. "This is Tori, the young woman I was telling you about. Tori, this is my mother, Julianna."

"Nice to meet you, Tori," the woman said.

Tori's neck craned back as she looked up at the woman. "You're sure tall," she said, then shook her head in embarrassment. "Sorry. You two don't look alike at all!"

"I'm adopted," Oscar said, glad that Tori had focused on the height difference, not her color.

"Really?" Tori asked. "Me, too. I mean, I just found out. How long have you known?"

"Pretty much forever. My parents bragged about it. 'Most parents are stuck with what they get. You were the pick of the litter' or 'We bought you off the top shelf' or 'You were the puppy with the cutest eyes.' Pretty much whatever hit them to say at the time. I think I must have heard a hundred reasons why they wanted me."

"Wow. I never thought of it that way," Tori said.

Oscar was distracted by a minor fracas at the front of the room. "Hey, Mom, could you hang on a minute? I need to scoot and see what all the excitement's about. Rich looks a little stressed."

"Sure. Tori and I'll be fine, won't we?"

Tori looked from the tall woman to where she thought her parents should be. Zip. They were gone. She sighed. She was mad at them for lying about who she was her all her life, denying her the sisters she knew were real. It was better to stay away from them right now. She probably wouldn't be able to hold back her rage.

She turned back to Oscar, "We'll be fine. She can tell me about France. I've never been there."

Julianna's smile slipped slightly. "Let's go over here where it's quieter," she said and headed to the table farthest from the commotion.

Tori followed. She'd never seen a woman so dark or so beautiful. She'd seen pictures of African Americans but had never met or seen one in person.

"You're going to hear about it sooner or later," Julianna began, skipping over the pleasantries and nonsense in case they were interrupted. "I was in a fancy nut house."

"Like Brazil nuts or Macadamias?" Tori asked, confused.

"No, like an insane asylum. People think I'm crazy. I'm not but all the medications they fed me had some pretty nasty side effects."

"Why would they think you're crazy? I mean, not to be presumptuous or anything, but people thought I was crazy, too." Tori said, then paused and leaned forward, eager to tell someone who might understand.

Julianna saw her excitement. "Go ahead. You first."

"You see, I *knew* there were two others just like me, that I had two sisters. No one had to tell me. I remembered them from before we were born. I remember everything. I didn't have proof until just a few minutes ago. My parents never mentioned it even though they must have known. I guess I should be glad they didn't feed *me* medications! I told a teacher and a friend about my sisters when I was in kindergarten. The teacher told my parents I would grow out of seeing and remembering others who weren't there. After that

122

conference, I didn't tell anyone. But still, my parents could have told me about them! Do you have sisters you see who the doctors tell you are just your imaginary friends, too?"

Julianna smiled at the innocent young woman her son was so fond of. Yes, she might understand. "No, not sisters. I was born in another time…"

Tori nodded but remained mute. Curious.

"Let me ask you a question first. Do you believe in time travel?"

"You mean like with the right equipment or starting from the right place, I could go backward or forward to another date?"

Julianna nodded, her bottom lip sucked in with apprehension.

"Duh!" Tori exclaimed. "Why not? I mean, just because we don't know how to do it today doesn't mean it isn't possible. Do you know people used to think the world was flat and the sun was the center of the universe? People were burned at the stake for believing stuff that we now know is true. Just because people hadn't figured out how to transmit sounds or knowledge through the air two hundred years ago didn't mean it wasn't possible. They just didn't have the right tools!"

Tori took the smartphone Oscar had given her out of her pocket. "Right now, I could just push a couple of buttons and talk to someone halfway around the world. How is time travel any different? If I had the right device, I could push a couple of buttons and be in 1776."

"Oh, my Lord! You are precious. You're not just saying this to humor me, are you?"

"No. I wouldn't do that," Tori said. She looked up and saw her mother approach. She stood up and waved, ready to forgive. "I'm over here."

Leanne bit off her admonishment about taking off and sat down next to her. What Oscar had told Luther was right. Tori was experiencing emotional growth spurts, this one right before her eyes. The once timid girl was interacting with strangers, not hiding in a coat rack.

Clink! Clink! Clink!

All three women looked at the podium. Roger Thornwhistle was trying to get everyone's attention, waiting for them to stop talking. "As the father of the bride, I'd like to thank all of you for coming. I see we have a few surprise guests tonight, too. It looks more like a family reunion than a wedding, but the bottom line is, we're family. Whether we were born into a family, legally adopted, or 'claimed,' I think everyone here is connected one way or another to each other. Here's to family!" he said, raising his champagne flute in toast. "Forever may we remember and love one another!"

"Here! Here!" and cheers answered his toast.

"Now, Chuck, you seem to be the instigator of about half of these reunions…"

"Or maybe all of them…" Chuck said with a sly smile.

"So, are there any more surprises you'd like to share?"

Chuck looked at the handsome man at his side and grinned. "Well, I guess one more to share with family won't break the scales. Ladies and gentlemen, I'd like to introduce my fiancé, Keith Fraser."

A handsome and slightly graying man eased himself out of his chair, red-faced and chagrined. "I guess there's no better way for Chuck to come out than among friends. For those of you who don't know, I was widowed a few years back. I didn't think anyone could fill that void, but Chuck did. We've known each other since college, but with one thing or another – including children for both of us and my marriage to John – we drifted apart. We'll wait for our children to be married first, but in the meantime, here's to love and family, and happy ever afters!"

"Mama, what's he talking about, marrying another man," Tori asked.

"Hush," Leanne said. "I'll let your father explain it to you later."

Tori looked over at her newly discovered sisters. Their faces were bright with happiness, clapping, whistling and cheering for Chuck and Keith and their announcement. "I guess that's another part of the world that's been kept from me for eighteen years. Looks like I have a lot of living to catch up on."

***

"So, are you going to stay mad at me forever?" Oscar asked Tori, keeping a cautious two feet away from her.

"Are *you* going to stay mad at me forever?" she replied and took a step toward him, closing the gap by half.

"I asked you first," Oscar said, grinning but not moving.

"I guess that depends on when you're coming home." She stepped forward, set her face into his chest, and inhaled deeply, hoping he'd hug her close. When he didn't, she looked up at him. "It was easier to be mad at you when you were far away, but right now…"

Oscar bent his knees and picked her up. He held her close, up high so her head was above his. "You have to tell me what's going on, what you want. I'm not a mind reader and you aren't either. I'm scared to death to hold you, kiss you, want you. Afraid that you'll shut me out again. Is that what you want?" He set her down and took a step back. "Because if you do…"

Tori jumped up and grabbed him around the neck, awkwardly placing a hard kiss that missed its target, the two of them clunking noses.

"Let's try that again," Oscar said. "I wasn't ready."

Tori's eyes lit up with a smile as bright as the bride's. "Prepare to be ready for me for the rest of your life!" She leaned in again, this time tilting her head to find her mark. When she finally pulled away from the kiss, she whispered, "Did I do that right?"

"I don't know. Let's try it again," he said and winked.

"That's enough, granddaughter," Silas said.

Tori pulled away quickly and Oscar released his hold, letting her slide to the floor in a controlled drop.

"I didn't mean to startle you," Silas said with a sly grin.

"Yes, you did," Tori said, then rolled her eyes and added, "Grandpa."

"Actually, it was my idea to come over to talk to you," Julianna

125

said, smiling at Tori, then patting her on the back with reassurance. "It looked like you two were having a serious discussion. We were going to wait, but then again, I didn't want you to get too carried away when you started using body language instead of words."

Oscar looked back and forth between his two favorite females. "I take it you and Tori found something in common? I mean, she generally isn't a very social person."

"Oh, we get along famously," Julianna said. She reached out and pulled Silas close by the elbow to join the family circle. "I wanted to talk to you before you two made too many plans for your future." She winked at Tori with the word 'future' and continued. "Silas and I have been chatting, too. It seems like we have a lot in common. He's a bit of a sleuth. He and I are going to North Carolina to do a little exploring in a month or two. In the meantime, we're going to be doing some research. In other words, you won't need to come back to France with me, Oscar."

"But…but…you just met him!" Oscar said.

"Actually, we knew each other a long, long time ago. We didn't recognize each other at first, but I think you two know how that is, right?"

"Mom…" Oscar asked, the concern in his voice evident. *Are you talking about that time travel nonsense again?*

Julianna saw the concern and said, "Don't worry about me. I'll keep in contact."

"Just make sure you have the right device," Tori said with a big smile and a wink.

"Absolutely!" Silas and Julianna said at the same time, looking at each other.

"That's my granddaughter," Silas said. "She's already got the hard stuff figured out."

The End

Note: This may be the end of Tori's story of finding her sisters and her true love, but it's just the beginning for Julianna and Silas. Watch for their story in *They Call Me Sherlock*.

Afterword

Would you like to know more about Chuck, Grace and Dusty, and all those wannabe grandpas? I intentionally went back in time to late 1991 and early 1992 to begin this saga. Here's a quick overview of the upcoming stories:

Vickie – Gloria and Roger's daughter – is dealing with lifestyles of the rich and famous in *Diamonds Aren't for Everyone*.

Rhianna learns about healing and life in *That Magic Touch*.

The Woodstock hippie botanists – Luther and Leanne – have their hands full with their spunky terror. *How Love Grows* follows Tori, a free-thinking independent sprite, as she tries not to fall in love with the new hand on her parent's marijuana farm.

The young woman Silas met at Woodstock in 1969 has shown up in his life again. Will they make a go of it? Will her secret ruin their possibility of a second-chance romance? *They Call Me Sherlock*.

Thanks for reading, and remember, authors love to get honest reviews!

About the Author

Author Dani Haviland started writing late in life and has been making up for lost time with a flood of works from sports, rom-coms, historicals, time travel, and Sweet and Sassy romances to Unforgettable romantic suspense and cozy mystery tales – with a few short stories thrown in to round out the reading experience. Dani is also the owner of Chill Out! Books, one of the publishers for The Authors' Billboard. Follow her on Amazon and BookBub to make sure you get her latest stories.

Contact information:

Website: www.danihaviland.com

Facebook: Dani Haviland Author and Dani Haviland & Friends

Readers Group: http://bit.ly/2DaniStTeam

BookBub: http://bit.ly/BBDani

Goodreads: http://bit.ly/2DHgdrds

Email: dani@danihaviland.com

Twitter: @dani_haviland and @gr8authors

I love to hear from readers!

Sign up for my newsletter to get the latest information on new releases, free stuff, and contests at: http://bit.ly/2DHnews

Other Books by Dani Haviland

ARLIE UNDERCOVER SERIES (romantic suspense based in Alaska and Arizona)

A Stingray Christmas: (Book One) Anchorage detective on medical leave travels from Alaska to Arizona to see for the first time the son he'd fathered as an anonymous sperm donor. Great and rotten surprises await the cop with the smartest smartphone around.

The Biggest Heart Ever: (Book Two) When would Arlie learn that trying to do everything by himself could be deadly—and make Charlene a widow before they were married?

Always a Bigger Fish: (Book Three) Back in Alaska, Arlie finds out he's a target. Will vacationing detective Billy Burke (from THE FAIRIES SAGA) have information to help nab the scalper?

How to Fix a Broken Life: (Book Four) When Arlie's very pregnant wife is kidnapped by pseudo terrorists, will he be the one to rescue her or will a surprise hero come in to save the day?

Because You Said So: (Book Five) Something's amiss at the Port of Anchorage. Will Arlie be able to solve it and still be back in time to wear the Santa suit?

Heaven and Heartbreak: (Book Six) How will Louie handle being a daddy? And what about that baby momma?

TRIPLETS: THREE AREN'T ONE

The Set Up: (Book One) Grace's story. How it all began with the mother from hell.

Diamonds Aren't for Everyone: (Book Two) Vickie's story – Growing up a billionaire.

That Magic Touch: (Book Three) Ria's story – Doctoring in the backwoods with secrets.

How Love Grows: (Book Four) Tori's story – Growing up in vineyards and marijuana farms.

They Call Me Sherlock: (Book Five) – Back to Woodstock with a friend.

THE FAIRIES SAGA SERIES
(historical fiction/time travel, listed in order):

Kibbles and Bits: FREE ebook: Sample the first stories in the series before you buy. The Fairies Saga stories. Find out how the first five books got their crazy names, too.

Naked in the Winter Wind: (Book One) How does an older woman wind up as a young hottie in Revolutionary War era North Carolina? First book in the time travel series.

Ha'Penny Jenny: (Book Two) More about the naïve and psychic young girl who was adopted into a time traveling family. Will her past catch up to her?

Aye, I am a Fairy: (Book Three) Young British lord finds himself entwined with a time traveling family and must decide if he should go back in time, too.

Dances Naked: (Book Four) Directionally challenged time traveler is rescued by Cherokee in 18th century. What must he do before the chief will show him to The Trees, the portal through time?

Chasing Christmas: (Book Five) A young Cherokee is rescued from an abusive man and changes the lives of many in this 18th century America family.

The Great Big Fairy: (Book Six) Very tall Benji grew up in the 20th century but was born in the 18th. When he finds a way to return to his grandparents in the distant past, he goes for it. Once there, he realizes he can't stay, but must return to the future.

Little Bear and the Ladies: (Book Seven) What's a bachelor trapper to do with all the females he rescues from the Hessian mercenaries? He'd better hurry and figure something!

Little Drummer Boy: (Book Eight) Young Scout works to earn money for a home in post-Revolutionary War America but runs up against prejudices and snowstorms.

Never Too Young: (Book Nine) Scout and Ha'Penny Jenny have grown up, but will they be able to spend their life together, or will the past and ruffians get in their way?

Time in a Little Blue Bottle: (Book Ten) Elvis, Mark Twain, and the prime vampire are racing to get the bottle of Fountain of Youth water before sweet Bella and the youthful pickpocket. So why are time travelers Marty Melbourne and Master Simon interested?

Kidnapped!: (Book Eleven) Benji's sister has been abducted and he and his Scottish police officer brother-in-law will do anything to get her back...even trust the mysterious letter sent by an ancestor, a convict on The First Fleet into Australia!

Big Mac: (Book Twelve) Can Big Mac stop his sire, the errant Viking time traveler, from starting a pandemic?

BENJI, THE LOST YEARS
(contemporary novellas about a young Benji MacKay)

Pool Boy Wanted: No Experience Preferred: (rather racy) Young Benji has been a hostage and slave, but life gets worse when an older woman decides she wants him as her own.

Luke the Unexpected: Love of classic motorcycles brought them together, but Luke and Holly have other challenges to face. Find out how their friend Benji got his stripes here.

STAND ALONE NOVELLAS *(contemporary romances)*

Kit Kringle: An Alaskan Tale: Kay moved to Alaska for the wrong reasons, then decided to stay and start her own business. What she hadn't planned on were prejudices and falling in love.

Be My Angel: Wyatt's dream to help save the wild mustangs began with the purchase of a rundown ranch in western Oregon. What he hadn't anticipated was being mesmerized by a sassy woman in a wheelchair.

Three Are One: The post chaplain tried to help the young widow adjust, but would his feelings for her and the search for his lost sister cause problems?

One Arctic Summer: That unforgettable summer of 1994 in Barrow, Alaska, and the touch she never forgot…If she goes back, will he remember her?

The Polar Xpress: Will the California chiropractor get a first chance at romance with the owner of Second Chance Kennels when he is stranded in Alaska?

Too Fast For You: Ten years after Little League, two talented professional baseball players wind up on the same minor league team. Will she remember him? And will their friendship be ruined if she does?